Henry Stephens Salt

A Shelley Primer

Henry Stephens Salt

A Shelley Primer

ISBN/EAN: 9783337388126

Printed in Europe, USA, Canada, Australia, Japan

Cover: Foto ©Andreas Hilbeck / pixelio.de

More available books at **www.hansebooks.com**

A
SHELLEY PRIMER.

BY

H. S. SALT.

LONDON:
REEVES AND TURNER, 196 STRAND.
1887.

Ballantyne Press
BALLANTYNE, HANSON AND CO.
EDINBURGH AND LONDON

PREFATORY NOTE.

———◆———

MUCH of the information given in the following pages is
drawn from the Prefaces and Notes to Messrs. Forman's
and Rossetti's editions of Shelley's works, and from the
critical and biographical writings of other Shelley students.
I am especially indebted to Mr. C. Kegan Paul and Mr.
W. M. Rossetti for their kind advice and many valuable
suggestions.

H. S. S.

CONTENTS.

———

SHELLEY PRIMER.

—✦—

CHAPTER I.

STATE OF ENGLAND IN SHELLEY'S LIFETIME.

Politics.—The period of thirty years (1792–1822) in which the life of Shelley was cast was a time at once of innovation and repression, of fierce conflict between governors and subjects, of strong popular movements on the one side, and equally stern reprisals on the other. Towards the close of the eighteenth century the spirit of inquiry had been abroad, and there had been a great awakening of the nations, which had taken visible form in the declaration of American Independence and the French Revolution. The immediate effect of these heart-stirring events was to stimulate reformers, all the world over, to further exertions, and to inspire them with hopes, which to us seem Quixotic, of realising in the near future their most sanguine dreams of Liberty and Justice. Spain, Italy, and Greece were all preparing themselves for the coming struggle; while, in the New World, Mexico and the Spanish colonies were striving to break away from the mother-country's control. Ireland was in revolt in 1798, and after the passing of the Act of Union in 1800 the persistent rejection of the Catholic Relief Bill was the cause of prolonged agitation. Then came a time of disappointment and reaction. In England, where the horrors of the French Revolution had filled men's minds with misgiving, the Tories, with "alarm" as their watchword of government, now ruled supreme. The first quarter of this century has been described as "an awful period for any one who ventured to maintain Liberal opinions;" perhaps the gloomiest time of all was the Regency of the Prince of Wales (1811–1820), with which Shelley's literary career almost coincided. England was then governed by such men as Castlereagh the author of the "gagging bills;" Sidmouth, the Home Secretary, whose one idea of sound policy lay in "crushing sedition;" Eldon, the Lord Chancellor, for forty years the enemy of every sort of reform; and Ellenborough, the Chief Justice, who in the numerous state-prosecutions of those days did not scruple to strain the law to the utmost against the accused. Under this Government civil and religious liberty was for the time trampled under foot, while the social condition of the working-classes grew more desperate every year. The close of the war with Napoleon in 1815 failed to bring any relief, and the riots that took place in many parts of the country were suppressed with great severity, the Government even going so far as to employ spies, as in the case of the notorious Oliver, for the purpose of inciting the discontented workmen to violence, and then betraying them to the gallows, which were constantly in use. Yet such books as Paine's *Age of Reason*, Godwin's *Political Justice*, and Mary Wollstonecraft's *Vindication of the Rights of Women* had not in reality failed in their effect; in spite of every obstacle the revolution of thought was being gradually accomplished, while the wide popularity gained by the writings of Cobbett in England and Owen in America proved that the demand for political and social reform was intensified rather than extinguished by the harsh measures dealt out to the reformers.

Literature.—In literature, as in politics, it was an age of conflict and revolution. The monotonous tyranny of the "correct" school of poetry, of which Pope may stand as the representative, was giving way to a truer, simpler, more

natural style, of which Cowper and Burns were the fore-
runners and Wordsworth the first apostle.   Thus there
uprose a new generation of poets, who, in their regard for
the spirit rather than the letter of the laws of poetry, resembled the Elizabethans of old, and stood in strong contrast to
their immediate predecessors of the eighteenth century. Break-
ing through the trammels of formalism which had long been
held indispensable, they proved that it was possible to unite
the most passionate feeling to the utmost simplicity of expression, and a close study of man to a deep sympathy with
nature.   It was not to be expected that this literary revolution would be effected without a struggle; here also there
were periods of repression and reaction, and by the help of
such critics as Gifford and his *Quarterly* reviewers—the
Eldons and Ellenboroughs of literature—the champions of
the old system often found effective means of retaliating on
their opponents.   In such an age as this, the world, as
Leigh Hunt has remarked, " requires the example of a spirit
not so prostrate as its own, to make it believe that all hearts
are not alike kept under, and that the hope of reformation
is not everywhere given up."

CHAPTER II.

SHELLEY'S LIFE AND CHARACTER.

Life.—Percy Bysshe Shelley was born at Field Place, Horsham, Sussex, the seat of the Shelley family, on August 4th, 1792. He was named Bysshe after his grandfather, a vigorous but eccentric old man, who received a baronetcy in 1806. Sir Bysshe was twice married, and founded two families, the Shelleys of Field Place and the Shelley-Sidneys of Penshurst, who number Sir Philip Sidney among their ancestors. Timothy Shelley, the poet's father, who succeeded to the baronetcy in 1815, was an old-fashioned country gentleman, much in his element as Tory member for the borough of Shoreham, but ill qualified to understand the character of his son. The mother, whose maiden name was Elizabeth Pilfold, had great personal beauty and fair intellectual power, but little taste for literature. The poet was the eldest child ; there were afterwards born five daughters and another son. Shelley's childhood was spent at Field Place, where he delighted in certain mysterious passages and garrets, and in the society of a " great old snake " which haunted the lawn. At the age of ten he was sent to Sion House, Brentford, from which school he passed to Eton in 1804. Here his strange disposition and his refusal to fag caused him to be teased by his schoolfellows, who called him "mad Shelley" and "the atheist." He learnt the classics with rapidity, and wrote fluent, if not correct, Latin verses ; but his chief interest was in private study of chemistry and in translating Pliny's *Natural History*. The only instructor for whom Shelley felt any respect was Dr. Lind, a retired physician living at Windsor, the original of the Hermit in *Laon and Cythna*. Shelley did not leave Eton prematurely, as has generally been supposed, but stayed there till the middle of 1810, by which time he had completed his novel *Zastrozzi*. In October 1810 he went to University College, Oxford, where he became intimate with Thomas Jefferson Hogg, who afterwards recorded the events of their college career in his *Life of Shelley* (*vide* p. 126). Their stay at Oxford was cut short by the publication of Shelley's pamphlet on *The Necessity of Atheism*, which resulted in the expulsion of both Shelley and Hogg, March 25, 1811.

Shelley had been deeply attached to his cousin, Harriet Grove, in 1809, but their intimacy was now broken off on account of his religious opinions. His father refusing to receive him at Field Place, he lodged for a time in London at 15 Poland Street; but in May 1811 he came to terms with his father, who agreed to allow him £200 a year. His restless and discontented state culminated in his elopement with Harriet Westbrook, the daughter of the proprietor of a London hotel, in the latter part of August 1811, not on account of any deep love for Harriet, but from a chivalrous desire to protect her from real or supposed tyranny. It is probable that Eliza Westbrook, Harriet's elder sister, had a great share in the ill-advised marriage and its disastrous termination. Harriet herself was good-tempered and good-looking, but not intellectually fit to be Shelley's companion, while Eliza, who lived with them, certainly widened the breach between Shelley and his wife. The marriage took place at Edinburgh on August 28th, 1811, and Shelley and Harriet were afterwards joined by Hogg, who accompanied them to York, where Shelley found it necessary to break off his intimacy with Hogg on account of his advances to Harriet. The Shelleys accordingly proceeded to Keswick, where they made the acquaintance of Southey. Then followed the visit to Dublin (February 12 to April 7, 1812), of which the fullest descrip-

tion is given in M'Carthy's *Shelley's Early Life*.   After
issuing his Dublin pamphlets and addressing a meeting of
Irish Catholics, Shelley left Dublin and travelled through
Wales to Devonshire, where he settled awhile at Lynmouth.
Here his party was visited by Miss Hitchener, a lady of
advanced opinions, with whom he had corresponded for some
time, but whose society proved to be less agreeable than he
expected.   From Lynmouth the Shelleys went to Tanyrallt,
near Tremadoc, in Carnarvonshire, where Shelley took part in
raising subscriptions to save the earthworks across the Port-
madoc estuary.   Here a mysterious attack was made one
night on the Shelleys' house, but whether the attempted
"assassination" was a reality or an illusion has never been
satisfactorily determined.   In May 1813 the Shelleys returned to London, where Ianthe Eliza, Harriet's first child,
was born some time in June.   In the summer of 1813
Shelley took a cottage at Bracknell, Berks., where he had
the society of the Newtons, a vegetarian family with whom
he had become intimate in London; a friendship which
influenced him strongly towards the adoption of certain
humanitarian views which seemed very ridiculous to his
friends Hogg and Peacock.   Mrs. Newton was the sister of
a Mrs. Boinville, whom Shelley greatly liked.   Towards the
end of 1813 an estrangement already existed between Shelley
and Harriet, owing partly to their growing divergence of
tastes, and partly to graver causes, it being Shelley's belief
that Harriet had been unfaithful to him.   In the early
months of 1814 Shelley spent much time at Mrs. Boinville's
house at Bracknell, the final separation taking place in June,
when Harriet went with her child Ianthe to her father and
sister at Bath.   Towards the end of the same year, she gave
birth to a son, Charles Bysshe.   Although Shelley deliberately separated himself from Harriet, he did not, as has often
been wrongly stated, desert her, or fail to make due provision
for her wants; on the contrary, he continued to correspond
with her, visit her, and advise her, after the separation.

Mary Godwin, who was at this time in her seventeenth year, was the daughter of William Godwin and Mary Wollstonecraft, and inherited great intellectual powers from both parents. Shelley did not know her till May 1814, and it was not till after the separation from Harriet that they pledged their love by the grave of Mary Wollstonecraft in St. Pancras Churchyard. On July 28th Shelley and Mary left England in the company of Miss Clairmont, a stepdaughter of Godwin, henceforth a frequent inmate of Shelley's family. Their tour on the Continent, which lasted till September 13th, was described by Mrs. Shelley in the *History of a Six Weeks' Tour.* During the closing months of 1814 Shelley was in London, much troubled by debts and creditors, but on the death of his grandfather, Sir Bysshe, early in 1815, his annual income was increased to £1000, and he became immediate heir to the entailed estate, though he had sacrificed his prospect of inheriting a still larger property by his refusal to agree to a further entail. The summer of 1815 was spent at Bishopsgate, on the skirts of Windsor Forest, where *Alastor* was written. After the birth of William, their eldest son, January 24, 1816, Shelley and Mary started with Miss Clairmont on their second Continental tour (May to September, 1816). At Sécheron, near Geneva, they met Byron, with whom Shelley made a trip round the lake. "Monk" Lewis was another acquaintance at Geneva, and it was under his influence that Mary Shelley then wrote her novel *Frankenstein.* Soon after his return to England Shelley received news of Harriet's suicide in the Serpentine, on, or soon after November 9th, 1816. During the last few months of her life she had sunk into lower and lower degradation, and the immediate cause of her suicide was remorse at being turned from her father's door. On December 30th, 1816, Shelley was married to Mary in London, and early in 1817 they settled near their friend Peacock at Marlow, where they stayed a year, a period fruitful in literary work, including *Laon and*

Cythna. A daughter, Clara, was born September 3, 1817. After the death of Harriet her father had refused to give up the two children, and took proceedings in Chancery to deprive Shelley of their control, the result being that Lord Eldon's judgment was given against Shelley in March, 1817, and the children were handed over to the care of a Dr. Hume. The boy died in 1826; Ianthe afterwards became Mrs. Esdaile. This loss of his children, next to Harriet's suicide, affected Shelley more deeply than any other misfortune of his life.

For various reasons, notably the state of Shelley's health, Shelley and Mary left England for Italy, March 11, 1818, again accompanied by Miss Clairmont. After first visiting Milan, the Lake of Como, Pisa, and Leghorn, where they met the Gisbornes, they settled for a time at Bagni di Lucca. On August 17th Shelley left Mary at this place, and visited Byron at Venice (vide *Julian and Maddalo*). He was afterwards joined by his family at I Capucini, a villa belonging to Byron at Este, where they stayed till November 5th. Their daughter Clara died on September 24th. They next travelled to Naples, spending a few days at Rome on the way, and arriving at Naples early in December 1818. They stayed there three months, Shelley suffering much from ill health and dejection during this winter. In March 1819 they returned to Rome, where their son William died on June 7th, and was buried in the Protestant cemetery. At Rome Shelley wrote the greater part of *Prometheus Unbound* and commenced *The Cenci*. Shortly after William's death Shelley and Mary went to Leghorn, where they stayed in the Villa Valsovano, and saw much of the Gisbornes. In September they went on to Florence, where their last child, Percy Florence, was born, November 12, 1819. At Florence, as at Rome, Shelley passed much time in the picture-galleries. In January 1820 Shelley and his wife left Miss Clairmont at Florence and settled at Pisa, where they made a lengthy stay, broken at times by visits to Bagni di Pisa and Leghorn, and enjoyed more congenial society than at any time since they left England. In the autumn of 1820 they were visited by Medwin, and about the same time they became acquainted with Emilia Viviani (vide *Epipsychidion*). Early in 1821 they met Edward and Jane Williams, with whom they soon became intimate friends. In August 1821 Shelley visited Byron at Ravenna, and discussed the plan of starting a magazine in conjunction with Leigh Hunt; Byron shortly afterwards came to Pisa, where he spent the winter in a house near that occupied by Shelley. Lastly, in January 1822, "Captain" Trelawny arrived at Pisa and saw much of Shelley during the last six months of his life. On April 26th, 1822, the Shelleys, with the Williamses and Trelawny, took up their abode in the Casa Magni, a solitary house on the shore of the Gulf of Spezzia, near Lerici. A great part of Shelley's time was now spent on board his small yacht, named the "Ariel," or in writing *The Triumph of Life*. The summer was sultry and foreboded storms, and some strange portents are said to have startled the small circle of friends at the Casa Magni. On July 1st, Shelley sailed with Williams to Leghorn, and greeted Leigh Hunt, who had just arrived in Italy. On Monday, July 8th, Shelley and Williams, with their sailor boy, Charles Vivian, started from Leghorn on their return voyage at 3 P.M. The afternoon was very hot, and a thunderstorm presently burst on the sea, during which the "Ariel" disappeared in the haze. When the storm cleared off, all traces of the yacht were lost; but she was found two months later in fifteen fathoms water, with the appearance of having been run down by a felucca during the squall. Whether this was due to accident or design will probably never be ascertained; there is, however, some slight ground for supposing that the boat was purposely run down by some Italian sailors, under the impression that Byron was on board with a large sum of money. Shelley's body was found, July 22, on the Tuscan coast, and buried

in the sand.   On August 16th it was burned, according to
the Italian law, the heart remaining unconsumed.   The
ashes were buried in the Protestant cemetery at Rome.

There are several points in Shelley's life which have never
been satisfactorily cleared up, and in which it seems impossible
to distinguish between fact and fiction.   Among these may
be mentioned his idea in boyhood that his father meditated
sending him to an asylum and was only restrained by Dr.
Lind's intercession; his statement as to his being expelled
from Eton and afterwards permitted to return ; the detailed
account of the attempted assassination at Tanyrallt; the
story of the mysterious lady who followed Shelley from
England to Naples and died there; the assault made on
Shelley by some unknown Englishmen at the post-office at
Pisa; and the dreams and visions recorded during the last
residence at the Casa Magni.   The frequent allusions to
drowning in Shelley's writings are very remarkable.   He is
stated to have said that shipwreck was "a death he should
like better than any other."   "If you can't swim, beware
of Providence," is Maddalo's warning to Julian ; and we
note that Shelley, who never learned to swim, was in danger
of drowning on several occasions before the final catastrophe,
viz., during the first voyage to Dublin; in crossing to Calais
in 1814; with Byron on the Lake of Geneva in 1816; and
in his light skiff on the Arno in 1821.   One or two anecdotes
told by Trelawny touch on the same point.   (Cf. *Alastor*,
lines 304, 305 ; the final stanzas of *Adonais, Ode to Liberty*,
and *Lines written in Dejection near Naples;* and a striking
passage quoted in *Shelley Memorials*, p. 126.)

After Shelley's death his widow, as we see from her poem
The Choice, reproached herself for her supposed coldness and
neglect, but it would be easy to take such reproaches too
seriously.   In spite of her dissimilarity to Shelley in
character, notably in her liking for society and greater
respect for conventionalities, she was well suited to be his
companion, and their affection and mutual respect were deep

and lasting. During the last period of their married life some misunderstanding arose between them, which drove Shelley to seek relief in the society of Edward and Jane Williams (*vide* the poem *To Edward Williams, The Magnetic Lady*, &c.). These misunderstandings were not due to Shelley's feelings for Emilia Viviani and Jane Williams, which indicated rather his craving after the ideal perfection of love, and certainly implied no loss of affection for Mary. But it seems that the affairs of Claire Clairmont, with whom Mary latterly often disagreed, had a disturbing influence on their household, and led to a temporary lack of sympathy between Shelley and Mary (*vide* Dowden's *Life of Shelley*, ii. 470). Mrs. Shelley returned to England in 1823. She edited editions of Shelley's works in 1824, 1839, 1840 (*vide* p. 120), besides writing several works of fiction. Her father, William Godwin, died in 1836; and in 1844, on the death of Sir Timothy Shelley, her son succeeded to the baronetcy. She died in London, February 21, 1851, and was buried at Bournemouth.

Character.—When Shelley's character is judged by the usual standard of morality, many of his opinions and actions, which from his own point of view were justifiable and conscientious, must necessarily appear strange and reprehensible. Love was at all times his dominant quality, and it is remarkable how all his intimate friends, although differing widely from him and from each other in opinions and disposition, bore united testimony to this moral beauty. His prominent traits were a rare unworldliness and an ardent enthusiasm; he felt that he had a mission to perform, and that he was charged with a message to his fellow-men. His generosity alike to friends and strangers was as munificent as it was unassuming, while his unselfishness in all the minor details of life was equally striking. His impulsive nature, chivalrous to a fault, was shown in his impatience of every sort of authority in which there could be any suspicion of tyranny, and in the culpable recklessness with

B

which he took up and "wore as a gauntlet" the name of "Atheist" (cf. his use of the term "Assassin" in the romance of that title; his representation of the serpent as the emblem of good; and the relationship of Laon and Cythna). Not less conspicuous, however, was the gentleness which made him shrink from all violence and cruelty, whether inflicted on man or the lower animals; the purity of mind which prompted him to resent any coarse or vulgar utterance as "blasphemy against the divine beauty of life;" the simplicity of taste which renounced the luxuries and self-comforts of the class to which he by birth belonged. "As perfect a gentleman as ever crossed a drawing-room," was Byron's remark on Shelley. Yet he was absolutely free from all class prejudice and aristocratic pride; the connection with Sir Philip Sidney, with whom he has often been compared in character, being the only link in the family genealogy which he cared to recall. His restless and mercurial temperament was another distinctive feature; at no period of his life had he what could be called a permanent home, but like the Wandering Jew, who figures so often in his writings, he roamed from place to place and settled nowhere. His dislike of ordinary society was very marked, but he delighted in the intellectual converse of friends and in argumentative encounter. His chief failing, especially in his earlier career, was his inclination to form his judgments of other men by his own standard; this constantly led him into a position of antagonism and disappointment, when he attempted to advance his doctrines in quarters where success was wholly impossible. In one sense he was certainly dreamy and unpractical, and by his forgetfulness of times and seasons he was ill qualified to be an inmate of an ordinary household. Yet it is a great error to suppose that he was altogether deficient in practical force and energy; on the contrary, what he said to Trelawny, "I always go on till I am stopped, and I never am stopped," was distinctly true of his character in some particulars. The shrewd determination he showed in publishing his juvenile writings gave an early proof that he was not wanting in that capacity for business matters which was afterwards to be made still more evident in some of his letters from Italy; while his practical kindness to the poor was long remembered at the places he visited. It was rather his dissimilarity to other men than any inherent inaptitude for business that made him seem visionary and unpractical; there was an elemental and primeval simplicity about his nature, which renders the expression "the eternal child," applied to him by Gilfillan, a peculiarly appropriate one. Yet it is not fair to argue that because he died young Shelley's opinions were merely crude and immature; for life and experience are not measured only by time. "If I die to-morrow," he himself said on a memorable occasion, "I have lived to be older than my father;" while, years before, in the *Notes to Queen Mab*, he had spoken of "the life of a man of virtue and talent who should die in his thirtieth year" as being by comparison a long one.

Habits.—It was Shelley's habit to rise early, study or write in the morning, and spend the evening in talking with his friends or reading aloud his favourite authors. He was seldom without a book in his hand, and it is related that he used to read even in a crowded London thoroughfare. The number of books that he read with his wife was very large; one or the other was almost always reading aloud. Next to reading, love of boating was his strongest passion; it is not quite clear whether he acquired this at Eton, or during an excursion up the Thames in 1815, but he was constantly on the water at Geneva and Marlow, and again in Italy. His habit of floating paper boats is amusingly described by Hogg and Peacock, and is referred to once or twice in his own writings (vide *The Assassins*, ch. 4, and *Letter to Maria Gisborne*, lines 72–75). When Byron and Shelley were together at Venice and Ravenna, riding and pistol-practice were their daily amusements, Shelley being an indifferent horseman but a good shot. One of Shelley's peculiarities, noticed by Hogg, was his habit of falling asleep on the hearth-rug with his head exposed to the full glow of the fire; we read also that in Italy he would bask bare-headed in the full heat of an Italian summer. His practice of vegetarianism was adopted early in 1812, and maintained, though not with entire consistency, during the rest of his stay in England. In his later years in Italy he to some extent gave it up, less from any change of principle than from the inconvenience caused to the household. But at all times bread was practically his staff of life, and his inclination was always to the simplest diet. He drank tea, but not wine. His habit in early life of beginning a correspondence with strangers deserves a passing mention. In this way he introduced himself to Felicia Hemans, Leigh Hunt, Godwin, and others.

Personal Appearance and Health.—Shelley was tall and active in figure, though he was slightly built and stooped considerably. His features, though not regular, were singularly expressive, and retained to the last their youthful aspect and almost feminine grace. His head was very small, and thickly covered with wavy dark-brown hair, which began to turn grey at an early age. His eyes were blue, with a fixed and earnest expression that gave the appearance of short sight. His voice was peculiar, being very high-pitched in tone, especially in moments of excitement, when, according to some of his biographers, it became "excruciating." At other times it was capable of pleasant modulation, both in conversing and reading aloud. It has been well remarked that both his appearance and voice were keen and high-pitched in harmony with his general character. Of the two original portraits of Shelley one was in oil, done by Miss Curran at Rome in 1819, and one in water-colours, by Edward Williams, done probably in 1821. From these two Clint composed a portrait after Shelley's death, and both this and the original by Miss Curran have been engraved and re-engraved. According to Mrs. Shelley's authority, Miss Curran's portrait is the better one; on the other hand, Trelawny preferred that by Clint. Exception has been taken, however, to all the extant portraits, as not giving a true likeness of Shelley, for the spiritual and ever-varying expression of his features rendered the task a very difficult one. Mulready said that he was "too beautiful" to paint.

Mrs. Shelley spoke of her husband as a martyr to ill-health, and his own statements were to the same effect, but some doubt has been thrown on this by Hogg and other writers. It seems certain that Shelley at times suffered great pain from nervous spasms, though he had intervals of good health. In 1815 he had consumptive tendencies which threatened to be serious, but these had passed away by 1818. It is less clear what was the nature of Shelley's malady during the last few years of his life. At Pisa he consulted the famous Italian physician, Vaccà, who at first thought that the disease was nephritis, but afterwards changed his opinion.

Shelley's Friends.—Thomas Medwin, Shelley's second cousin, was one of his schoolfellows at Sion House. He afterwards corresponded regularly with Shelley, and visited him in Italy in 1820 and 1821. (On his *Life of Shelley, vide* p. 125.)

Thomas Jefferson Hogg was Shelley's intimate friend at Oxford. An estrangement arose between Shelley and Hogg after Shelley's first marriage, but they afterwards saw much of each other in London, and Hogg is more than once mentioned with affection in the letters from Italy. In his early life Hogg was to some extent in sympathy with Shelley, though latterly of a cynical turn of mind. In 1826 he married Edward Williams' widow. (*Vide* p. 126.)

William Godwin had corresponded for some months with Shelley before they met in London, October 1812. After the elopement with Mary in 1814, Shelley's relations with Godwin were much strained, and it was not till the end of

1816, when the marriage with Mary took place, that a reconciliation was effected. In later years Shelley gave Godwin
much pecuniary assistance.

Leigh Hunt became intimate with Shelley in 1816, their
friendship ripening apace during that year and the following,
as Hunt was perhaps the most sympathetic of all Shelley's
friends. They met again for a few days at Leghorn and
Pisa immediately before Shelley's death. "To see Hunt is
to like him," Shelley wrote in 1820, and this feeling was
reciprocated by Hunt. Shelley's liberality to his friend was
unbounded.

Thomas Love Peacock became acquainted with Shelley in
1812, and visited him at Bishopsgate in 1815, when they
went on a boating excursion up the Thames. They were
intimate at Marlow in 1817, and some of Shelley's best
letters from abroad were written to Peacock. Shelley
greatly admired his writings, and liked him personally, but
Peacock's cynical disposition rendered him unable to appreciate Shelley's best qualities. "His enthusiasm is not very
ardent, nor his views very comprehensive," Shelley wrote to
Hogg. (*Vide* p. 126.)

Lord Byron first met Shelley in 1816 at Geneva; then at
Venice in 1818, at Ravenna in 1821, and again at Pisa
during the last year of Shelley's life. Byron had a liking
for Shelley, and highly respected his character; but though
their friendship was cordial, they were never on a footing of
perfect ease. Shelley was justly indignant with Byron on
account of his treatment of Claire Clairmont, but he greatly
admired his genius. (Vide *Julian and Maddalo*, p. 59.)

Horace Smith was introduced to Shelley by Leigh Hunt in
1817, and afterwards managed some business matters for
him during his absence in Italy. Shelley speaks of him
warmly in his *Letter to Maria Gisborne* and elsewhere.

John Keats also met Shelley at Leigh Hunt's house. He
did not respond very cordially to Shelley's friendly overtures,
and seems to have scarcely appreciated the genius of his

fellow-poet. In July 1820 Shelley invited Keats to join him at Pisa. (Vide *Adonais*, p. 70.)

The Gisbornes became intimate with Shelley and Mary at Leghorn, where they had a house. Mrs. Gisborne taught Shelley Spanish. (*Vide* p. 113, and *Letter to Maria Gisborne*, p. 66.)

Edward Ellerker Williams and his wife, Jane, were introduced to the Shelleys by Medwin at Pisa, in January 1821. Williams had been in the navy, and rivalled Shelley in his fondness for the water; Jane Williams was very musical, and delighted Shelley by her singing. They lived near the Shelleys at Pisa, and shared the Casa Magni at Lerici. Shelley was much attached to Williams, and his affection for Jane inspired some of his most beautiful lyrics of 1821 and 1822.

Edward John Trelawny, Shelley's latest but not least intimate friend, had travelled in many parts of the world and led a romantic seafaring life, which lent a considerable charm to his society. In spite of the contrast in their characters and the short period of their acquaintance, he understood Shelley better than some of his earlier friends. After the death of Shelley and Williams, the duty of arranging for the burning of their bodies and the subsequent burial of the ashes fell on Trelawny. (On his *Records of Shelley*, vide p. 125.)

Local Records.—*Field Place.*—An engraved plate, with an inscription, has been placed over the fireplace in the room where Shelley was born.

Eton.—There is no visible record of Shelley at Eton, the school authorities having hitherto discountenanced any attempt to class him among the Eton "worthies." The house in which he boarded was pulled down about twenty-five years ago.

Oxford.—Shelley's rooms at University College, in the corner of the quadrangle, near the hall, are now known as " the Shelley lecture-room."

Keswick.—Chestnut Cottage, where Shelley stayed in 1811, is still in existence.

Marlow.—An inscription has been placed on the outer wall of the house where Shelley lived. It records, incorrectly, that Shelley was there visited by Byron.

Rome.—The following is the inscription on Shelley's grave in the new Protestant cemetery at Rome :—

PERCY BYSSHE SHELLEY,

COR CORDIUM,

NATUS IV. AUG. MDCCXCII,

OBIIT VIII. JUL. MDCCCXXII.

"Nothing of him that doth fade
But doth suffer a sea-change
Into something rich and strange."

The relics of Shelley's heart, which Trelawny rescued from the funeral-pile, are preserved at Boscombe, Sir Percy Shelley's residence, together with the manuscripts of his works, the Sophocles clasped in his hand when he was drowned, and other memorials.

CHAPTER III.

SHELLEY'S OPINIONS.

(1.) **Philosophical and Religious Opinions.** *Doctrine of Necessity.* — Shelley's first inclination was towards philosophy rather than poetry, a preference which he again expressed as late as 1819 in a letter to Peacock. It is suggested by Mrs. Shelley that, had he lived longer, he might have written a "complete theory of mind;" as it stands, however, his philosophy is by no means consistent throughout. In early life he was imbued with the materialism of the French school, and the doctrine of necessity is strongly urged in the *Notes to Queen Mab* (*vide* p. 103), though this, as has often been pointed out, can scarcely be reconciled with the enthusiastic moral exhortations and the belief in the power of the will which pervade most of his poems, *Queen Mab* included.

Idealism. —But his mind, as it has been truly said, "possessed an original bias towards Transcendentalism," and he soon became discontented with the cold and colourless tenets of materialism. By about 1815 he had adopted the immaterial philosophy of Berkeley, who asserted that nothing exists but as it is perceived, *i.e.*, matter itself is only a perception of the mind (*vide* essay *On Life*, p. 105). His Platonic studies confirmed this belief in idealism, and he must be considered, in his maturer years, as distinctly a Platonist and idealist in thought. In accordance with this philosophy he regarded as unreal and transitory all the phenomena of life and death, space and time, which can exist only as we think of them ; while he sought to grasp the one reality of thought, the inner *idea* which underlies all outer and material appearances (*vide* Ahasuerus's speech in *Hellas*, lines 766–806, for a succinct expression of this doctrine). It will be seen that in all Shelley's later writings, whether philosophical or poetical, the *ideal* is the dominant quality.

The Existence of Evil.—On this question Shelley held a kind of Manichean doctrine, which is very clearly expressed in *Laon and Cythna* (canto i., stanzas 25–33), and again, though less simply, in *Prometheus Unbound* (act ii. sc. 4). Evil is not inevitable in the nature of man : but from the beginning of all things there have been two rival, co-existing powers of Good and Evil, typified in *Laon and Cythna* by the serpent and the eagle, in *Prometheus Unbound* by Prometheus and Jupiter. These " twin Genii, equal Gods," maintain a ceaseless combat, in which, in spite of temporary defeat and suffering, the good will ultimately prevail. In short, Shelley firmly believed in the perfectibility of man by the power of the human will. This forms the subject of *Queen Mab, Laon and Cythna,* and *Prometheus Unbound.*

The Existence of a Deity.—Shelley's belief or disbelief on this point is not easy to define, but pantheism is probably the term most expressive of his views, since he certainly believed in a universal world-spirit pervading all substance (cf. *Adonais*, stanza 42, and similar passages). The ambiguous use of the name *atheist,* for which Shelley was himself primarily responsible, was the cause of considerable misconception of his religious opinions ; and it is to be regretted that he did not define more distinctly what meaning he attached to words of this class. In *Queen Mab,* for instance, and in most other places where he speaks of *God,* he evidently uses the name in the strictly theological sense, to denote the personal deity whose existence he denied. Yet there are a few passages in *Prometheus Unbound, Epipsychidion, Adonais,* and *The Boat on the Serchio,* where *God* seems to signify rather the soul of the universe, in which Shelley as certainly believed. He himself in his youth adopted the name of atheist, and appears not to have disowned it towards the close of his life ; but it should be remembered that he did this chiefly in a spirit of chivalrous defiance. The word atheist, in its present opprobrious sense, is not justly applicable to him ; for his atheism was simply a disbelief in the personal deity of orthodox theology.

Nature.—According to Shelley's pantheistic view, all nature, "from man's high mind even to the central stone of sullen lead," is animated by one eternal spirit, which underlies all passing phenomena. Man, himself a portion of nature, turns to her for comfort and guidance, recognising the beauty of her manifestations by the kindred emotion of his own heart; while nature in her turn sympathises with the joys and sorrows of man (cf. *Prometheus Unbound*, act iv.).

The Immortality of the Soul.—Shelley seems, like his master, Plato, to have been content to suspend judgment on this point, under the stress of two conflicting tendencies of thought. Medwin asserts that he believed in ante-natal life, and Hogg tells a story of his interrogating a new-born infant about its previous existence; but this idea is only incidentally referred to twice or thrice in the poems (cf. *Epipsychidion, Prince Athanase,* and *The Triumph of Life*), while it is discountenanced in the essay *On a Future Life.* As regards a future existence, the negative opinion, based on pure reason, is advanced in the last-named essay (*vide* p. 106) and other passages ; while the affirmative view, expressed as a hope rather than an argument, may be found in *Adonais, The Sensitive Plant,* the *Essay on Christianity,* and *The Punishment of Death.* In one of the *Notes on Hellas* Shelley says that the *desire* of immortality "must remain the strongest and the only presumption that eternity is the inheritance of every thinking being ; " and in some conversations recorded by Trelawny he expresses the same opinion. It was useless, he maintained, to dogmatise on a question which is quite insoluble. In the meantime he had no curiosity about the system of the Universe. "My mind is tranquil," he said; "I have no fears and some hopes." It therefore seems probable that Shelley was inclined to believe in immortality; not, however, in the sense of a separate individual existence, but rather a fusion of the individual mind in the universal.

Christianity.—His attitude towards Christianity was more clearly marked. He resembled Blake in the strong contrast of feeling with which he regarded Christ on the one hand, and the Christian religion on the other. For the "sublime human character of Jesus Christ" he felt the deepest respect and veneration, as may be seen from the famous chorus in *Hellas,* and the notes to that poem, the *Essay on Christianity, Letter to Lord Ellenborough,* and passages in *Prometheus Unbound.* But he repudiated and condemned in the strongest manner the dogmas of the Christian faith, and thought it a duty to utter his opinions plainly on the subject of the existing religion. "If every man," he wrote, "said what he thought, it could not subsist a day." He felt that the spirit of established Christianity was wholly out of harmony with that of its Founder, and that a similarity to Christ was one of the qualities most detested by the modern Christian; if a second Jesus should arise in these days, his fate would be "lengthened imprisonment and infamous punishment." That Shelley, whether right or wrong in his general view of Christianity, did scant justice to the inner force which determined its historical development, at any rate in its earlier stages, can scarcely be denied; but there is no warrant whatever for the strange theory propounded by several writers,[1] that under different circumstances he might himself have adopted the Christian tenets. His objections to Christianity were far too deeply rooted, and rested on too real a foundation, to admit

[1] *Vide* Browning's Introduction to *Letters,* published 1852; F. W. Robertson's Address to Brighton Working Men; Gilfillan's *Gallery of Literary Portraits,* &c.

of any such mental transition, unless we gratuitously suppose a total change in his nature, character, and habits of thought. This has been very clearly put by De Quincey in his essay on Shelley.

Again, in his mention of *faith*, which he calls an "obscene worm" and the "foulest birth of time," it must be understood that he means the faith of the theologian only; of faith in its fuller and wider sense he himself possessed no small portion. *Repentance* is another of the Christian virtues which he more than once condemns (cf. *Laon and Cythna*, viii. 22), but only in the special sense of that morbid self-abasement and useless brooding over the past which retard the omnipotence of man's will in the future. It is important to note these points, for Shelley did himself an injustice in here leaving some scope for ambiguity and misrepresentation. His hostility to Christianity as a religion was at all times characteristic and determined, but it was not that mere unreasoning antipathy, that "midsummer madness," with which he has been charged. His intimate knowledge and love of the Bible should alone be sufficient to refute that idea. So far from being, as he has often been lightly called, an ".irreligious" man, he was in the truest sense profoundly religious, though his faith was intuitive rather than traditional, and therefore could not harmonise with any established creed. He claimed for himself and for all others absolute freedom of opinion in religious matters, on the ground that belief and disbelief are equally involuntary (vide *Letter to Lord Ellenborough*, p. 102).

(2.) **Morals.** — The power of the human will, in other words, the perfectibility of man, is the cardinal point in Shelley's moral teaching. We might be wise and virtuous and happy, if we would but set aside the tyranny of custom, and allow scope for the intuitive excellence of our true nature; for original goodness, and not original sin, is the inalienable birthright of mankind. The foundation of true morality is therefore that innate benevolence which, together

with a sense of justice, is the parent of virtue.   At one time
Shelley meditated an essay on this subject, "to show how
virtue resulted from the nature of man," and holding this
opinion he condemned custom and compulsion of all kinds
as hostile to the essential conditions of virtue.   Kings and
priests are outlawed and anathematised, not on any foolish
supposition of their personal wickedness, but as being the
representatives of civil and religious oppression ; and, according to Shelley's doctrine, perfect liberty is absolutely indispensable to the existence of virtue.   "Gentleness, virtue,
wisdom, and endurance," are the four great moral qualities
on which Shelley insists ; while of the opposing vices,
tyranny, custom, and revenge are those that he most often
deprecates.   In the *Essay on Christianity* he quotes the
authority of Christ against "the absurd and execrable doctrine
of vengeance."   For Shelley's definition of Virtue, Benevolence, and Justice, vide *Speculations on Morals*, p. 106.

Love.—Love, which in Shelley's view is an almost equi-
valent term to Liberty and Nature, is the great power through
which the world may be regenerated.   This Love is represented under three aspects, between which it is difficult to
draw a very strict distinction, viz., the ideal, the personal,
the philanthropic.   The ideal Love is defined in the essay
On Love as the " soul within our own soul," the "something
within us, which, from the instant that we live, more and
more thirsts after its likeness."   It is the yearning after that
divine spirit which pervades the universe ; the recognition
of outward beauty by the corresponding inward ideal ; the
"Uranian Venus" towards which we must needs struggle,
though we often meet her counterfeit the "Pandemian
Venus," and in our quest for the ideal are disappointed by
contact with the actual (vide *Hymn to Intellectual Beauty*,
Alastor, Epipsychidion, Essay on Love, The Coliseum, &c.).
The subject of personal Love, though often merged into that
of the ideal, is treated with some directness in the lyrics,
especially the later love-songs.   Lastly, the philanthropic

Love is that spirit of unselfishness which Shelley considered to be the only remedy for all moral, social, and political evils; "the great secret of morals," he wrote, "is Love."

(3.) **Social Views.** *Necessity of Social Reform.*—In social as in moral regeneration, Love is to be the great motive power. "If there be no love among men, whatever institutions they may frame must be subservient to the same purpose—to the continuance of inequality." Starting from this principle, Shelley strongly condemns the present system of society, which, he says, "must be overthrown from the foundation, with all its superstructure of maxims and forms." His views are distinctly revolutionary and socialistic, not only in *Queen Mab* and its *Notes*, but in the whole body of his writings. The twenty-eighth *Declaration of Rights* runs as follows: "No man has a right to monopolise more than he can enjoy; what the rich give to the poor, whilst millions are starving, is not a perfect favour, but an imperfect right." He repeatedly insists that there is no real wealth but the labour of man, and that the rich are directly indebted to the poor for the comforts they possess; "the labourer, he that tills the ground and manufactures cloth, is the man who has to provide, out of what he would bring home to his wife and children, for the luxuries and comforts" of the rich. He "shuddered to think" that even the roof that covered him and the bed on which he lay were provided from the same source. Under these conditions the boasted freedom of Englishmen was little better than a delusion; there can be no true freedom where there is poverty and want (cf. *Masque of Anarchy*, stanzas 39–56). It is no wonder that Owen should have spoken admiringly of the holder of these opinions, or that *Queen Mab* became, as Medwin tells us, the gospel of the Owenites. For a remedy for these social evils Shelley looked to the growing sense of disinterestedness and justice; he had little faith in political economy, or the doctrines of Malthus, but he hoped that a reformed Parliament might see the necessity of abolishing the National

Debt, and investigating the claims of all fund-holders. Neither, on the other hand, did he trust to mere legislative changes, still less to any violence or force, being of opinion that all reform is useless unless accompanied by a corresponding self-improvement. "Reform yourselves," is the keynote of the *Address to the Irish People*, and the same warning is enforced in the *Essay on Christianity*, where the failure of the early Christian socialism is attributed to the fact that it preceded that moral improvement from which it ought rather to have resulted. For this reason simplicity of life is frequently inculcated by Shelley; to decrease his own physical wants is the duty of every earnest man, for he "who has fewest bodily wants approaches nearest to the divine nature." The world has enough, and more than enough, of science and inventions and mechanical skill; but it is sadly deficient in generous impulse, unselfishness, and the poetry of life ; hence has resulted "the abuse of all invention for abridging and combining labour, to the exasperation of the inequality of mankind." (The passages where Shelley's social views are most clearly stated are in *Notes to Queen Mab, Address to the Irish People, Declaration of Rights, On Christianity, On the Death of the Princess Charlotte, Letters from Italy*, and the unpublished *Philosophical View of Reform*.)

The *Emancipation of Woman* is another of Shelley's great social themes. He painted in glowing colours the happiness that might result if women could burst the bonds of restraint imposed on them by ignorance and custom, and stand forth as the free and equal companions of men. In *Laon and Cythna* this vision is presented in its fullest form ; Cythna being the type of the perfect woman, at once the tender and gentle comforter, and the swift and fearless liberator. In *The Cenci* we note the same spirit in Beatrice, though warped and repressed by the pitiless conditions of her life. In *Rosalind and Helen* he deals with the subject of the social degradation of woman, though in a less direct and powerful manner than in *Laon and Cythna*. Shelley's views on the marriage-laws are well-known from the famous *Note to Queen Mab* (*vide* p. 103), and a passage in *Epipsychidion*. He regarded the marriage-bond as disastrous both for woman and man, while the inconsistency in his own practice was due solely to the desire of shielding the woman from what is at present regarded as a social disgrace.

Humanitarianism.—Shelley's humanitarian opinions are generally passed over as an amiable eccentricity, but in reality they form a very characteristic and necessary part of his moral teaching. He condemns war as a criminal and foolish practice in the *Address to the Irish People,* and capital punishment was equally incompatible with his doctrine of gentleness (*vide* p. 105). He deprecated cruelt and violence of all kinds; and his vegetarianism, as set forth in his *Vindication of Natural Diet,* and *Laon and Cythna* (canto v.), and referred to in *Alastor* and the *Refutation of Deism,* was no mere fastidious crotchet, but directly connected with his belief in universal Love. He was too large-hearted and clear-minded to be able to restrict his benevolence to mankind alone, or to view with equanimity the sufferings of the lower animals (*vide* p. 104).

(4.) **Politics.**—We find the axioms of Shelley's political opinions in the *Declaration of Rights* and *Speculations on Morals.* "Politics are only sound when conducted on principles of morality." "The basis of all political error" is inability to recognise that unselfishness is intuitive ; that it is wiser to promote the happiness of mankind than to consider self or class-interests, although this fact cannot be mathematically proved. Shelley was an ardent reformer and republican, and if his early zeal was somewhat modified in his later years, there is no reason to suppose that his convictions were altered. He regarded political freedom as a necessary means to an end, for only the free can be just and wise. He therefore advocated the extension of the franchise in his *Proposal for Putting Reform to the Vote* (*vide* p. 108). *Catholic Emancipation* is demanded in the *Address to the*

C

Irish People, while in the *Proposals for an Association* he
suggests a method of obtaining this result and also the
Repeal of the Union (*vide* p. 101). After leaving England,
Shelley continued to take great interest in public affairs, as
may be seen from the group of political poems of 1819 (*vide*
p. 96), which he intended to work up into a regular series,
and many of his letters testify to the same political watch-
fulness (cf. the *Philosophical View of Reform,* 1819, p. 109).
He expected national bankruptcy, as well as revolution,
and considerately warned his friends, the Gisbornes, who
had invested in English funds, that their ruin was demanded by "justice, policy, and the hopes of the nation."
But though his heart was entirely with the popular party,
he always insisted strongly on the necessity of caution and
moderation.   Laws, however bad they may be, must not
be resisted by force, for a good cause can only be injured by
employing violence ; it is right to protest, but it is not right
to rebel.   This characteristic doctrine of a passive protest is
fully developed in the *Masque of Anarchy* (stanzas 74–90).
Caution is also recommended in the *Proposals for Putting
Reform to the Vote* about the method of extending the
franchise and abolishing royalty.   In political matters, as in
moral, Shelley earnestly deprecates a policy of vengeance ; in
Peter Bell he deplores the tendency of the poor to take
"Cobbett's snuff, Revenge."

Shelley had a strong dislike to party politics and the nar-
row views of newspapers ; his own opinions being thoroughly
cosmopolitan : "The only perfect and genuine republic is
that which comprehends every living being." His sympathies
with all oppressed nations were intense, and he watched with
the keenest anxiety the outbreaks in Spain, Italy, and Greece,
1820–1821 (vide *Ode to Liberty, Ode to Naples, Hellas,* &c.).
In the preface to *Hellas* he remarks that England's true
policy should be to maintain the independence of Greeks
against both Turks and Russians.   There is a fine tribute to
America, the "home for freedom," in *Laon and Cythna*

(xi. 24), and again in the last scene of *Charles the First*, while the constitution of the United States is spoken of with approval in the *Philosophical View of Reform*.

(5.) **Literature and Art.**—Shelley's views on these subjects may be gathered from his *Defence of Poetry ;* Prefaces to *Laon and Cythna, Prometheus Unbound*, and *The Cenci ; Letters from Italy*, and *Notes on Sculpture*. The scope of art is to portray the impression made on man in his contact with nature and society, poetry being the most direct method of doing this. The function of poetry, as an art, is to quicken the imaginative powers, and not to convey any direct teaching. Didactic poetry was Shelley's " abhorrence," though he did not shrink from enlisting his poetical powers in the cause of reform. The catholicity of his literary tastes is shown by his enthusiastic admiration for the Old Testament, Æschylus, and Calderon, writings of a style very different to that of the Revolution. In Italy his few chosen books consisted of the Greek Plays, Plato, Lord Bacon, Shakspere, the Elizabethan dramatists, Milton, Goethe, Schiller, Dante, Petrarch, Boccaccio, Machiavelli, Guicciardini, Calderon, and the Bible. In contemporary literature he preferred Byron's *Cain* and *Don Juan*, the odes of Coleridge, some of Wordsworth's early poems, and Landor's *Gebir*. As a critic, however, he was hardly in his element ; his delight in giving pleasure causing.him to praise too much ; as appears from his criticisms on the writings of such friends as Godwin, Leigh Hunt, Peacock, Hogg, Medwin, and Williams ; while he was too apt to idealise and exaggerate the merits of any book that fascinated him.

Shelley's appreciation of the fine arts was dormant till roused by the treasures of Rome and Florence, where he studied intently, jotted down the *Notes*, and wrote long descriptive letters to Peacock, more valuable for literary style than any correctness of art-criticism. He seems to have disliked Michel Angelo, and to have had an exaggerated admiration for Guido and Salvator Rosa, being attracted probably by the sentiment of the former and the energy of the latter. At Pisa he had no opportunities of continuing these studies.

Before concluding this chapter it may be worth while to consider to what writers Shelley is most indebted for the suggestion of thoughts and opinions. Among philosophers he constantly mentions Plato and Lord Bacon as holding the highest rank—the antipodes to Paley and Malthus. The influence of Plato is very strong throughout all Shelley's ideal poetry, especially in the doctrine of love (cf. *Epipsychidion*) ; he was also inspired by Rousseau in a smaller degree. On the other hand, in all ethical and political questions of the day he was a follower of Godwin. He himself says that Godwin's *Political Justice* materially influenced his character. His opinion that no punishment is justifiable, except as correction for the sake of the culprit, and that the death-penalty is therefore objectionable ; that all laws, especially the marriage-law, are mischievous, though for other reasons it may be necessary to conform to them ; that property belongs justly to him who needs it most ; that all coercion, even in education, does harm rather than good ; that unselfishness is the only true guide in political and social life ; all this, together with the doctrine of passive protest and abstention from violence, was inspired by the writings of Godwin. Mary Wollstonecraft's *Vindication of the Rights of Women* doubtless inspired much of Shelley's ardour in that cause.

CHAPTER IV.

LITERARY CHARACTERISTICS.

Ideality.—The dominant characteristic of Shelley's poetry is its ideality. He constantly endeavours to penetrate the outer cloak of appearances and grasp the *idea*, the reality that underlies all forms; what he strives to depict is therefore not so much the actual object perceived by the senses, as the idealised image of it, apprehended only by the mind. Whether he is preaching a crusade of social liberty and free thought, as in *Queen Mab, Laon and Cythna*, and *Prometheus Unbound ;* or of national and political freedom, as in *Hellas*, the *Ode to Liberty*, and *The Masque of Anarchy ;* or eulogising the poetic character, as in *Alastor* and *Adonais ;* or singing of love, as in *Epipsychidion ;* or the imaginative faculty, as in *The Witch of Atlas*,—we find always the same ideal treatment of the subject on which he writes.

Subjectivity.—Next to his ideality, subjectivity is Shelley's most important quality. He is one of the most subjective of poets, many of the characters in his longer poems being idealised portraits of his own, and the most beautiful of his short lyrics being direct outpourings of his own emotions. With the single exception of *The Cenci*, where he was compelled to curb this tendency, it would be difficult to point to any important poem by Shelley which is not to some extent subjective.

Nature-Worship.—Another marked feature is his sympathy with nature, which may be traced in his many descriptions of skies, dawns, sunsets, clouds, storms, forests, flowers, mountains, caves, seas, and rivers. Shelley told Trelawny that "he always wrote best in the open air, in a boat, under a tree, or on the banks of a river;" and his poems have accordingly much of the vitality and elementary freshness of nature itself. He may claim to share with Wordsworth the title of "Poet of Nature," for his treatment of natural scenery is not the less true because it is idealised, and instinct with passionate adoration and love, rather than careful thought and patiently diligent observation (*vide* p. 27).

Varieties of Style.—The scope of Shelley's literary powers was far wider than is usually supposed; to think of him as a lyric poet only is to make a very common but very complete mistake. The versatility of his genius was shown in the following ways. (1.) *Lyric poetry*, as befitting a subjective writer, was certainly the element in which Shelley was most at ease; in passionate fervour of imagination and melody of language he is generally admitted to be unsurpassed. Out of his many odes, songs, and lyrical pieces there are very few that do not reach a high standard; and his later lyrics are masterpieces of beauty and simplicity combined. He is at his best in those metres which allow free play for sustained imaginative flight; in the more artificial metres, such as the sonnet, he is not often successful. (2.) As a *dramatist* Shelley relies for fame on *The Cenci* and the fragment of *Charles the First*. Dramatic power was precisely what one would least have expected to find in a writer of Shelley's temperament. In a letter of 1818 he himself remarks: "You will say I have no dramatic talent; very true in a certain sense; but I have taken the resolution to see what kind of tragedy a person without dramatic talent could write." The success of *The Cenci* is indisputable; yet it may fairly be urged that this is in great measure due to the happy choice of subject; a struggle against parental tyranny being a theme specially suited to Shelley's genius. When in his *Charles the First* he attempted to deal with history, "that record of crimes and miseries," as he elsewhere described it, he could not make the same progress, and the drama remains a fragment, though too fine a fragment to be set down as a failure. Whether Shelley could ever have produced a series of great dramas, must therefore remain under debate. As it is, he can scarcely be called a great dramatist, though he has the merit of having produced the greatest drama of modern English literature. (3.) *Narrative poetry* in the ordinary sense was perhaps Shelley's weakest point; his attempts in this direction, as seen in parts of *Queen Mab, Alastor, Rosalind and Helen*, and even *Laon and Cythna*, lack directness and concentration. On the other hand, in the familiar-narrative style of *Julian and Maddalo* and the *Letter to Maria Gisborne*, he is at his strongest and best. A study of these two poems, where simple incidents are touched on with inimitable grace and versatility, yet with a firm and steady grasp, should suffice to dispel the notion that Shelley's genius was entirely visionary and transcendental. (4.) Shelley's position in *satirical* writing, as in dramatic, is difficult to define with any certainty. Satire was not quite congenial to his gentle and kindly spirit; and the question of his humour, or lack of humour, is still an open one. Humour is the quality of which enthusiasts are proverbially devoid; yet in Shelley's case it seems to have been latent rather than absent; for though many of his works are conspicuously destitute of it, we see it very plainly in *Peter Bell*, the essay *On the Devil and Devils*, and some passages of some of the poems and letters. The wit in *Swellfoot* is rather laboured and ponderous; and perhaps it may be said that while some of Shelley's humorous pieces are far from unsuccessful, we feel that this style of writing was rather against the grain. (5.) As a *translator* Shelley had great qualities. He was well aware of the difficulty, or rather impossibility, of reproducing the melody of another language, but he strove to make his versions true English poems; one of his canons of work being that "translations are intended for those who do not ˉunderstand the original, and therefore should be purely English." In spite of occasional mistakes, due to carelessness or ignorance of idiom, he seldom fails to catch the spirit of his originals, though he is not careful to follow them in metre. His translations were generally thrown off at a time when he felt unfit for original writing, as a secondary occupation on which he placed little value. In his translations from the ancient languages the Greek largely predominates, for Shelley cared little for Latin, and looked on the Romans as " pale copyists " of the Greeks, for whom his admiration was unbounded. He is said to have learnt the Classics almost by intuition. In modern languages he translated from the Italian, Spanish, and German, but not from the French, for which literature, one or two writers excepted, he had a strong dislike. He had studied Italian with Hogg in 1813, and he afterwards read much with Mary in Italy. Considering his familiarity with Italian literature, we are surprised Shelley did not translate more. For his introduction to the Spanish tongue Shelley was indebted to the Gisbornes (*vide* p. 23); there is a conflict of evidence as to when he became acquainted with German, but it was probably not until 1815. (6.) As a *prose writer* Shelley was at his best in some of the essays and the letters from Italy. His boyish Romances are entirely worthless, except as a proof of his early determination to make his mark in literature. The earlier essays and pamphlets are remarkable for vigour and keen logical insight rather than weight, and except in the *Essay on Christianity, Defence of Poetry*, and a few other masterpieces, the literary style of the essays has been affected, perhaps unavoidably, by the polemical nature of the subject-matter, a fault which is also discoverable in the earlier letters. But in the letters written during the last few years of his life, his ease and mastery are at once apparent; as in the "poetic-familiar" vein of *Julian and Maddalo*, so too in his familiar prose correspondence he strikes the golden mean between the over-

elaborate style of the last century, and the practical but
somewhat inartistic method of his contemporaries. The
descriptive letters may be regarded as a kind of prose-poetry,
suggested by the same impulses as many of the poems, and
written, like them, under the immediate stress of inspiration.
They give a view of the conditions under which the poems
were composed, and thus indirectly afford a proof of their
sincerity in thought and style. Medwin tells us that Shelley
used to write his letters on his knees during intervals at
meals, "his pen flowing with extraordinary rapidity, and his
mind mirrored on the paper."

Favourite Subjects, Images, and Words.—The repetition
of certain images and words is one of Shelley's most marked
characteristics. Among metaphors frequently used are
those drawn from the instruments of weaving, the warp,
woof, and web; from a lyre or Æolian harp hung up to the
wind; an eagle and serpent locked together in fight. The
references to serpents are very numerous, and perhaps owe
their origin to the "great old snake" that haunted the
garden at Field Place. In the first canto of *Laon and
Cythna*, and elsewhere, the serpent is used by Shelley to
represent the spirit of good; but often also in the contrary
sense. "The Snake" was the nickname given to Shelley
by Byron. Boats and rivers furnished another common
theme, the "little shallop" playing an important part in
Alastor, as also in *Laon and Cythna, The Witch of Atlas*,
and many other poems. Flowers and plants are often mentioned, as in *The Question, The Sensitive Plant*, and *The
Zucca*, while the sky, with all its shifting scenery of clouds
and storms, was ever present in Shelley's imagination. Of
human characters, that of the ideal Sage or venerable Al-
chemist figures in *The Coliseum, Laon and Cythna*, and *Prince
Athanase*, as an exception to the usual tyranny of Age; and
still more common is the "Youth with hoary hair," doubtless meant in some measure for Shelley himself. Perhaps
the strangest instance of Shelley's recurrence to a favourite

idea is in his references to Ahasuerus, the Wandering Jew. One of the juvenile poems dealt with that story; and the same character appears in *Queen Mab* and its *Notes*,—where the legend is told at some length,—*Alastor*, *Hellas*, and *The Assassins*. Here too should be mentioned the quotation "*Letting I dare not wait upon I would*," which recurs with odd persistency in Shelley's writings. As a typical example of the repetition of a particular image, it may be noted that the description of the reflection of a city quivering on a river's surface appears in at least four passages, viz., *Ode to Liberty* (stanza 6), the lines on *Evening* (1821), *Witch of Atlas* (stanza 59), and *Ode to the West Wind* (stanza 3). *Lair, den, dœdal, moonstone, hyaline, nursling, windless, anarch*, are instances of words that Shelley is fond of using.

Metre.—*Blank verse* is used in *Queen Mab, Alastor, Prometheus Unbound, The Cenci, Swellfoot, Hellas*, and some of the translations, with great mastery and success. With the exception of Keats, Shelley has scarcely a rival in this metre among modern English poets. In parts of *Queen Mab* we find unrhymed lyrical iambics, as in Southey's *Thalaba*. The following are the chief rhymed metres used by Shelley. The *Spenserian Stanza*, revived by Byron, appears in *Laon and Cythna* and *Adonais*. Shelley's stanzas are not so compact and forcible as Byron's, but have greater fluency and grace, the number of double rhymes being a noteworthy feature. The *Heroic metre* is that of *Julian and Maddalo, Epipsychidion, Letter to Maria Gisborne, Ginevra*, and some shorter pieces. In Shelley's hands it becomes free, unfettered, and familiar, recalling the "mighty line" of Marlowe rather than that of the eighteenth century school. The *seven-syllabled trochaic*, the metre of Milton's *L'Allegro* and *Il Penseroso*, is a favourite with Shelley; e.g., *Euganean Hills, The Invitation, Ariel to Miranda, Lines at Lerici, The Masque of Anarchy*, some of the lyrics in *Prometheus Unbound*, and some political poems and translations. The *iambic tetrameter*, the metre of Scott, is less common, but is found in parts of *Rosalind and Helen*. The *ottava rima* is used with rare skill and delicacy in *The Dream, The Zucca, Witch of Atlas*, and translation of *Hymn to Mercury;* while the intricacies of the *terza rima*, that most difficult of metres for an English poet, are wonderfully handled in *Prince Athanase, The Woodman and the Nightingale, The Triumph of Life, Ode to the West Wind*, and a translation from Dante. The lyric arrangements used by Shelley are far too numerous to mention. The Sonnet he seldom attempted, and only once or twice with success. Most of his sonnets are loosely constructed, and in some cases the usual sonnet-laws are completely set at defiance.

Rhythm and Rhyme.—In language and power of expression Shelley is rich almost to excess, his teeming fancies finding a ready outlet in the inexhaustible flow of words. He could use alliteration freely without abusing it, and a treasury of metaphorical imagery was always ready to his hand. He wrote at a white heat of passionate inspiration, and this lyric fervour was one cause of his frequent neglect of so-called " rules of poetry ; " correctness of particular rhymes being unhesitatingly sacrificed to the general musical effect. Such half-rhymes as *nest, east ; move, love*, are frequent on every page ; and we occasionally meet with more questionable aberrations, such as *accept not, reject not ; frost, almost ; leaves, peace ; ruin, pursuing ;* and many instances (especially in *Laon and Cythna*) of such loose rhyming as *motion, emotion ; fell, befell*. It has been remarked that Shelley's poems are never unrhythmical, though the rhyme and metre are sometimes at fault. In some cases the charge of metrical defect is due to not recognising that Shelley often deliberately chose an unusual cadence, as in the line " And wild roses and ivy serpentine ; " or purposely suppressed one syllable for the sake of the effect, *e.g.*, " Is it with thy kisses or thy tears ? " " Fresh spring, and summer, and winter hoar." Signs of haste and inaccurate workmanship, where they exist, must be attributed partly to the eagerness of poetic inspiration and the profusion of images and ideas, partly to the moral enthusiasm which pervades most of the poems ; it must be remembered also that Shelley regarded mere artistic perfection and elaborate style as of distinctly secondary importance. It may be fairly urged that the fragmentary state of so many poems and essays is a sign of desultory work ; this was caused in some measure by his solitary life in Italy, where he lacked the encouragement of literary society ; also, no doubt, by the restless and transitory impulses of his own nature. Shelley was always and essentially the poet of youth, and, together with its fervid hopes and yearnings after an ideal justice and love, he possessed somewhat of its restlessness and lack of repose. This appears as plainly in his literary style as in his life and character. Just as Wordsworth's writings are full of tranquillity and sober contemplation, so Shelley's breathe the spirit of zeal and activity. He represents a particular phase of thought and feeling, which, though not universal, has special charms at certain periods and for certain natures.

Mysticism.—Another charge often brought against Shelley's style is that of obscurity and lack of human interest. That occasional lines and passages are very obscure, there can be no question, but the obscurity is generally only a verbal one, or caused by some corruption of the text. In the Myths, however, which Shelley handles in *Prometheus Unbound* and elsewhere, his love of allegory and metaphysical subtleties occasionally renders the meaning difficult ; while the unexplained personal allusions in *Epipsychidion, Julian and Maddalo,* and some other poems are less pardonable blemishes. But as a rule it may be said that the general sense of Shelley's writings is lucid and well-expressed ; though of course his meaning is more likely to escape those who are unaccustomed to his line of thought, than those who are in sympathy with him. The same explanation will apply to his so-called want of human interest. It is true that he does not deal, as Wordsworth does, with simple, homely incidents of everyday life, yet no writer has ever been more in earnest in the cause of humanity, and the powerful interest of his writings is strongly felt by readers of a kindred disposition, though others may remain unmoved by it. He was, in fact, the poet-prophet of the future, and his vistas of thought are therefore of necessity somewhat vague, vast, and spiritual; but though the outline, like a landscape by Turner, may be misty in detail, there is no obscurity in the general effect.

Plagiarisms.—The "plagiarisms" of Shelley are, as Professor Baynes has remarked, "psychological curiosities rather than serious blemishes." Shelley's mind was naturally receptive, and it is not surprising that from his multifarious reading he should sometimes have unconsciously appropriated the thoughts and even the words of other writers. In the Preface to *Prometheus Unbound* he admits that the study of contemporary writings may have "tinged his composition;" but it is evident that he was quite unaware of the extent to which he had absorbed favourite images and cadences from old poets as well as new. In the Preface to *The Cenci* he is careful to acknowledge a debt to Calderon as the only plagiarism he had intentionally committed, though in reality there are others quite as striking; while in *Alastor* he assigns inverted commas to the Wordsworthian phrase "too deep for tears," but not to "natural piety" and "obstinate questionings." *Queen Mab* shows traces not only of Southey but of Pope, Gray, Collins, Akenside, and Thomson; *Alastor* is deeply tinged with the influence of Wordsworth; *Laon and Cythna* has many echoes of Spenser; and *The Cenci* often recalls passages in *Othello*, *King Lear*, *Macbeth*, and other Shaksperean plays.

Grammar.—Shelley's grammar, owing to his hasty style of composition, is at times slipshod and defective. We meet with such solecisms as "like *thou*," "let you and *I* try," "*these* sort," "to *lay*" (for *lie*), "to imprecate *for*," &c. The past participle is sometimes used loosely, and there is often a confusion about the 2nd person sing. of the verb, *e.g.*, " thou lovest, but ne'er *knew*." Another kind of error where a plural verb follows a singular noun (*e.g.*, " the shadow of thy moving wings *imbue* ") was probably caused by the présence in Shelley's mind of the plural "wings ; " a similar mistake at the beginning of the Preface to *Adonais* may be accounted for in the same way. (Comp. also a passage in the *Lines written among the Euganean Hills,* lines 40–43, and the strange phrase " *those* deluded crew " in *The Triumph of Life.*) It was characteristic of Shelley to care less for grammatical accuracy than the general sense ; but it seems scarcely necessary to suppose that he purposely sacrificed grammar to euphony.

His usual though not invariable method of spelling some words was peculiar, but apparently deliberate : *e.g.*, desart ; ætherial, etherial ; recal ; extacy, ecstacy ; falshood ; knarled ; stedfast ; tyger ; &c. (*vide* Appendix to Forman's edition). He sometimes adopted the phonetic style, as in " vext."

Archaic words. — Many archaic words borrowed from Chaucer, Spenser, Shakspere, or Milton, are used by Shelley, especially in *Laon and Cythna.* Among these are *blosmy* (blossomy) ; *undight* (dishevelled) ; *thwart* (cross-grained) ; *forbid* (accursed) ; *brere* (briar) ; *crudded* (curded) ; *besprent* (besprinkled) ; *teint* (tint) ; *sill* (seat) ; *swink* (labour) ; *foison* (plenty) ; *frore* (frozen) ; *griding* (cleaving) ; *grain* (dye) ; *prankt* (variegated) ; the obsolete plurals *eyne* and *treen ;* and the past tenses *glode, strook, clombe. Uprest* in the sense of uprising (noun) occurs in *Laon and Cythna,* being apparently adapted from Chaucer's *upriste.* The German *griff* (grip) was oddly introduced by Shelley into *The Sensitive Plant.*

CHAPTER V.

LITERARY PERIODS OF SHELLEY'S LIFE.

I. **Juvenile Period** (1808–1811).—The love of the marvellous was Shelley's ruling passion at this time, his imagination running freely on " bandits, castles, ruined towers, wild mountains, storms, and apparitions," while his favourite authors were Southey and M. G. Lewis. His chief juvenile works were the two romances, *Zastrozzi* and *St. Irvyne* (*vide* p. 114); the poem on *The Wandering Jew, Original Poetry, by Victor and Cazire,* and *Posthumous Fragments of Margaret Nicholson* (*vide* p. 79). Besides these, Shelley wrote also a number of short pieces, which are included in Rossetti's and Forman's editions. It is said that many of these were printed at Horsham at the expense of Sir Bysshe Shelley. None of those extant are of any literary value ; and the worthlessness of Shelley's juvenile writings is their most conspicuous feature.

II. **Propagandist Period** (1811–1814).—This is the true beginning of Shelley's literary career, the tract on *The Necessity of Atheism* marking his first serious effort. The romances now give way to pamphlets and propagandist writings, and the prose predominates largely over the poetry. The chief works of this period are *The Necessity of Atheism, The Irish Pamphlets,* the *Letter to Lord Ellenborough, Notes to Queen Mab,* and *A Refutation of Deism* (*vide* p. 101–104). The only poems of any note are *The Devil's Walk* and *Queen Mab.* Some of these writings are occasionally classed with Shelley's *juvenilia ;* but, with the exception perhaps of *The*

Devil's Walk, they are distinguished from the real *juvenilia* above mentioned by their greater earnestness of tone and increased power of expression. The doctrines advanced are often sound in their main purport, even where the actual application is foolish and unseasonable; and though it would be futile to deny the great superiority of the later productions, it would be equally unjust to class *The Irish Pamphlets* or *Queen Mab* with the puerilities of *St. Irvyne* or *Margaret Nicholson*. It will be observed that this second period coincides with Shelley's life with Harriet, during which he took up the gauntlet against custom and society in the too confident hope of effecting a speedy change.

III. **The Bishopsgate and Marlow Periods** (1814–1818) date from the beginning of Shelley's life with Mary Godwin to their departure for Italy. Experience had taught Shelley the folly of expecting immediate results from his doctrines; while the influence of Mary Godwin and the novelty of his travels on the Continent stimulated him to fresh efforts. There are now signs of wider sympathies with nature and man, and a vast improvement in descriptive power. Poetry begins to take precedence of prose; and though the essays are still mainly propagandist, it is noticeable that they are often fragmentary, as if Shelley were tiring of direct didactic writing. It is possible, however, that ill-health was the cause of this. *The Assassins* (1814) is an instance of Shelley's increased power. The Bishopsgate year (1815) was full of literary plans, *Alastor* being then written, and possibly also the *Essay on Christianity* and the group of essays mentioned on p. 105. The *Hymn to Intellectual Beauty* (1816) is also remarkable. The Marlow period (1817) was a very productive one, including *Laon and Cythna*, the two "Hermit of Marlow" pamphlets, and a number of short poems (*vide* p. 81).

IV. **The Italian Period** (1818–1822).—Shelley now withdrew to a more contemplative life in Italy, "the land of ideal scenery," where his genius could develop more freely, and in a more congenial climate; and we see accordingly that his natural bent towards the *ideal* henceforth dominates all his writings.   The didactic element is now finally withdrawn; prose is greatly reduced in scope, while poetry becomes all in all, the letters, which now appear as an important feature, being highly poetic in tone.   Shelley's opinions still remained unchanged; but they are henceforth expressed in a poetical rather than polemical method, as for instance in *Prometheus* and *Hellas.*   Latterly, however, the purely lyric and personal element was strongly in the ascendant, the short poems of 1821 and 1822 being remarkable for their extreme simplicity and directness.

In this period the prose writings are reduced to the *Defence of Poetry, Philosophical View of Reform,* the *Letters, Translations, Notes on Sculptures,* and some fragmentary essays; while no less than seven volumes of poetry were published between 1819 and 1822 (*vide* p. 119), and many other poems, lyrics, and translations were written, but not published till after Shelley's death (p. 120).   *Julian and Maddalo* and the *Lines written among the Euganean Hills,* both inspired by the visit to Venice, were the chief productions of 1818.   *Prometheus Unbound* and *The Cenci,* together with some of the finest lyrics, date from 1819, which may be regarded as the crowning year of Shelley's life.   The residence at Pisa, 1820 and 1821, witnessed the writing of a large number of poems, among which were *The Sensitive Plant, The Witch of Atlas,* the *Ode to Liberty, Hellas, Epipsychidion,* and *Adonais.*   The Bay of Spezzia, in 1822, was the scene of the last phase in Shelley's literary career; and here were written some of the most impassioned of the lyrics addressed to "Jane," and the great fragment on *The Triumph of Life.*

D

CHAPTER VI

THE POEMS.

I. Longer Poems. Ideal and Subjective.—The poems placed in this class are arranged in chronological order. It is impossible to draw any satisfactory line of demarcation between the ideal and subjective, as the two qualities are often combined by Shelley in the same poem (*vide* p. 37).

(1.) *Queen Mab.*—Shelley seems to have begun *Queen Mab* as early as 1809, and to have corrected and recast it in 1812, finishing it in February 1813, and then adding the *Notes*. In the same year he privately published an edition of 250 copies, which he sent to various friends and correspondents, among whom the poem made some sensation. In 1821 a piratical edition was issued by Clark, a London bookseller, to Shelley's great annoyance, as expressed in several letters. Since Shelley's death *Queen Mab* and its *Notes* have been several times republished, both in England and America, and have had a wider circulation than any other of his writings, considerably influencing the working classes in the direction of free thought. The metre of *Queen Mab* is unrhymed lyrical iambic, like that employed by Southey, interspersed with declamatory passages of blank verse. There is a poetical dedication *To Harriet ******, which Shelley himself mentions in a letter of 1821 as a reference to Harriet Westbrook, though it seems possible that it was first intended for Harriet Grove.

Summary.—The sleeping Ianthe is visited by Mab, the Fairy Queen (comp. the "Witch of Atlas," another personification of the imaginative power), who summons her soul to leave her body and ascend the magic car. They soar aloft, and reach the Temple of Nature, whence they survey with mental vision the empires of the old world, Syria, Egypt, Judæa, Greece, Rome, and Carthage, the "stately city" of the West. Ianthe thus learns the lessons of the Past, the mortality of man, and the vitality of the universe. Then follows a dissertation on the Present; the crime of kingship; the peace of nature broken by human wars; the tyranny of kings, priests, and statesmen; the selfishness of commerce; of all which evils Religion is the guilty cause (comp. the doctrine of Lucretius, a writer dear to Shelley even in boyhood). This leads to the praise of Necessity, the true deity. To explain still further, Ahasuerus (*vide* p. 42) is summoned, who, though himself only a creation of the fancy, can yet tell a tale to illustrate the guilt of a fanciful religion. Lastly the Future is foretold, as an age of bliss when all the world shall be fruitful, and nature and mankind at peace. The magic car then descends to earth; Ianthe's soul rejoins the body, and she wakes to find her lover watching by her side.

It will thus be seen that the Past, Present, and Future are the "comprehensive topics" of *Queen Mab*. It is a vehement attack on established religion and society, written at a time when Shelley's expulsion from Oxford was still fresh in his mind. In spite of its declared atheism it contains a strong element of the pantheistic doctrines afterwards developed by Shelley when he had outgrown the Necessity of *Queen Mab*. Its revolutionary speculations have made it the subject of much praise and much disparagement, some declaring it to be a great poem, while others allow it scarcely any merit. It is certainly vastly inferior to Shelley's true masterpieces; its arguments being confused and ill-arranged, with much repetition and ·unnecessary declamation, while the poetry lacks the peculiar music of Shelley's later verse. But many of the declamatory passages are exceedingly fine and sonorous, and the main conclusions advanced in the poem, however unpopular they may be, have not been disproved by time; it therefore seems scarcely justifiable to class it with the *juvenilia*, for if not a great work, it is distinctly a notable one. Shelley in after years wrote of it as "villainous trash," but as he was then vexed at the issue of the pirated edition, and as he had not seen the poem for several years, and "hardly knew what it was about," it is safer to judge *Queen Mab* on its own merits than by the author's opinion of it. In the last year of his life Shelley remarked to Trelawny that the matter of *Queen Mab* was good, though the treatment was unequal.

For *Notes to Queen Mab*, vide p. 103.

The Dæmon of the World may be here conveniently mentioned. Under this title Shelley published in the *Alastor* volume (1816) a variation from the first two sections of *Queen Mab;* and the recent discovery of the very copy of *Queen Mab* worked upon by Shelley in making this revision has brought to light a second part of the *Dæmon of the World*, made up from the concluding sections. The *Dæmon of the World* is interesting as showing what parts of *Queen Mab* Shelley cared to preserve; but it lacks the energy and the *raison d'être* of the original poem.

(2.) *Alastor; or, The Spirit of Solitude*, was written at Bishopsgate in the summer of 1815, and published with some shorter poems in 1816. There is a Preface by Shelley, and a quotation from St. Augustine's *Confessions* which strikes the keynote of the poem—the "love of love." The title, which was suggested by Peacock, means primarily an Avenging Spirit, and must be understood to refer to the Spirit of Solitude and not to the youth who is haunted thereby; though the latter interpretation is also permissible, according to the secondary meaning of the Greek word. We can trace in *Alastor* the influence of Shelley's wanderings amidst wild scenery, his reminiscences of Lucerne, the Reuss, and the Rhine, which he had visited the preceding year, and his present seclusion among the oaks of Windsor Park ; it is also "softened by the recent anticipation of death."

Summary.—After an invocation of Nature, the universal mother, the poet's story is told. He leaves his "alienated home," and wanders far through Athens, Tyre, Balbec, Jerusalem, Egypt, and Arabia, where he is tended by an Arab maiden, till he reaches Cashmere. Here he sees a vision of "a veiled maid," which banishes for ever his peace of mind. He wanders on, in search of this phantom love, to the "lone Chorasmian shore," where he finds a little shallop, and embarks. The boat is driven by a storm beneath the cliffs of Caucasus, through the long windings of a cavern, and stranded at last on the verge of a waterfall. Then follows a description of the forest scenery through which the poet roams, till he finds his resting-place in "a silent nook" and dies. The poem concludes with a wish that the secret of prolonged life, known only to "one living man" (Ahasuerus), could be attained by mankind.

The allegory is sufficiently explained in Shelley's Preface. The poet is at first happy in calm communion with nature ; but when he seeks a human embodiment of his vision of loveliness, he finds that his happiness is gone, the Spirit of Solitude has undone him. The "veiled maid" whom he vainly follows is the ideal love, unattainable in earthly form ; his error consists in seeking the earthly and actual instead of the heavenly and ideal. (Comp. *Hymn to Intellectual Beauty, Epipsychidion, The Zucca,* &c.) The poem is strongly subjective ; we feel throughout that the youthful poet is Shelley himself ; and the slightly morbid tone is accounted for by Shelley's state of health at the time. *Alastor* is written in blank verse of great beauty and strength, and is a distinct advance on *Queen Mab* from a literary standpoint, its descriptive passages ranking with some of Shelley's best work, while the aggressive optimism of *Queen Mab* is here temporarily replaced by the purely personal element. The text of *Alastor* is very corrupt in places, and there are some passages that almost baffle interpretation. For the poems published with *Alastor* in Shelley's original edition, *vide* p. 119.

(3.) *Laon and Cythna ; or, The Revolution of the Golden City*, usually known as *The Revolt of Islam*, was written at Marlow in the summer of 1817, and printed at the close of the same year. A certain number of copies, probably more than has generally been supposed, had already been issued, when the publisher, Ollier, took alarm at some passages of the poem, especially those treating of the relationship of Laon and Cythna, and insisted on delaying further publication until changes had been introduced. Shelley was compelled, much against his will, to assent to this ; the title was accordingly changed, the final paragraph of the preface omitted, and some fifty lines of the text revised and modified. It so happened that all this could be done by merely cancelling a few pages, and using the old sheets ; the poem was thus published in January 1818.

Laon and Cythna was written in the open air, partly among the Bisham woods, and partly on the Thames. The love of natural scenery is strongly stamped on every page ; while Shelley's hatred of human tyranny was intensified by the Chancery suit, which deprived him of the care of his children in the spring of that year. The subject of *Laon and Cythna* (Laon from Greek λαος, a people), which is stated at some length in Shelley's Preface, was the emancipation, in poetic vision, of Islam (*i.e.*, the nations of the Levant), whereby the "Golden City" is liberated for a time from the Sultan's yoke ; but it must also be understood in a wider sense as typical of the struggle between the principles of free thought and conventional morality (comp. *Hellas*). The Spenserian stanza was chosen as more suitable than blank verse.

Summary.—The dedication " *To Mary* —— —— " (Mary Wollstonecraft Shelley) is a piece of poetical autobiography, describing Shelley's first awakening in his schooldays to the

higher life (either Sion House or Eton is referred to, probably the former; vide *Hymn to Intellectual Beauty*); his
loneliness until he met with Mary Godwin; and their subsequent happiness. There is a reference in stanza 12 to the
death of Mary Wollstonecraft. *Canto I.* is introductory.
The poet tells how he witnessed a contest between the eagle
and serpent (emblems of tyranny and free thought), and how
the wounded serpent took refuge with a woman "beautiful
as morning" (the spirit of nature and love). She invites the
poet to accompany her in her boat; and as they sail, tells
him of the eternal struggle between the two powers of Good
and Evil; also the story of her own life, in which there
may possibly be a reference to the personality of Mary
Wollstonecraft; which would account for the otherwise puzz-
ling statement that she is "a human form," and the mention
of her visit to Paris at the time of the Revolution. Thus
they reach the Temple of the Spirit, where sit the "mighty
Senate" of the dead, to join whom two spirits (*i.e.*, Laon
and Cythna) have just arrived. *Canto II.* Laon is now the
speaker. He describes his youth and early resolutions at
Argolis; his love for his little sister Cythna ("orphan" was
substituted in *The Revolt of Islam*), and their determination
to liberate the Golden City. *Canto III.* Laon and Cythna
are suddenly seized by the soldiers of the tyrant, Othman;
Cythna is carried into captivity, and Laon is chained to a
lofty column, where he is rescued from death by the Hermit
(*vide* p. 11). *Canto IV.* The Hermit carries Laon to his
tower, where, after a madness of seven years, he recovers;
and hearing of a revolution in the Golden City, brought
about by a mysterious maiden, he sets out thither. *Canto V.*
describes the peaceful triumph of the revolutionists. The
tyrant himself, with his daughter (who afterwards turns out
to be the child of Cythna), are befriended by Laon. The
liberated people rejoice round the "Altar of the Federation,"
where Laone (Cythna) sings her triumph-song of Wisdom,
Love, and Equality, which is followed by a bloodless feast.

Canto VI. The tyrant's troops attack and treacherously massacre the citizens. Laon, resisting with a few followers, is rescued by Cythna on her Tartar steed, and they escape to a ruined castle, where they pledge their love. *Cantos VII., VIII., IX.* Three cantos are now devoted to Cythna's account of her life since she was parted from Laon. She tells him of the tyrant's harem ; a mysterious cave to which she was taken by a diver ; the birth of her daughter, who was afterwards taken from her ; and her escape on a slave-ship. (The narrative here leaves us in some doubt whether Othman or Laon is to be regarded as the father of Cythna's daughter. There is some countenance for the latter view in Cantos vii. 18, xii. 24 ; but on the whole the former seems more probable.) Her eloquence had induced the seamen to set the captives free ; and, on reaching the Golden City, she had begun her revolutionary crusade. Here her story ends, and Laon recommences. *Canto X.* The plague which followed the massacres is now described. As an expiation, the priests doom Laon and Cythna to the funeral-pile. *Canto XI.* Laon, after leaving Cythna at the castle, appears in disguise before the tyrant, and reveals his name, on condition that Cythna is allowed a safe passage to America. *Canto XII.* Cythna, however, arrives, and shares Laon's death. As they die the tyrant's child also falls lifeless. They awake after death, and are greeted by the child-spirit, Cythna's daughter, who guides them in her pearly boat down a mighty stream to the Temple of the Spirit mentioned in the introductory canto.

Shelley was careful to state that *Laon and Cythna* is a narrative, not didactic poem ; it is nevertheless a return from the somewhat morbid " self-seclusion " of *Alastor* to the more vigorous enthusiasm of *Queen Mab.* It is the epic of free thought, free love, and humanity in the widest sense ; and in no other English poem is the emancipation of woman preached with such earnestness and force. Yet it is also subjective in a high degree ; Laon, like the two other characters sketched at Marlow, Athanase and Lionel, being a portrait of the poet himself; while Cythna is Shelley's ideal of womanly perfection, gentle, frank, eloquent, and full of tender pity for all suffering and grief. *Laon and Cythna* is the crowning effort of Shelley's career in England; it has great merits, but it has also corresponding faults. For lofty sentiments, gorgeous imagery, and subtle melody, it could scarcely be surpassed; yet, as Shelley himself admits in a letter to Godwin, there is "an absence of that tranquillity which is the attribute and accompaniment of power." The polemical cast of the poem could not but be fatal to artistic repose; it consists, in fact, of a brilliant "succession of pictures" rather than a perfect work. The plot of the narrative is vague and loose in the extreme, and sometimes, as in the first part of Cythna's story (canto vii.), recalls to our mind the fantastic and incredible conceptions of Shelley's early romances. The Spenserian stanza is wielded with much grace and fluency, but not with the same uniform mastery as in *Adonais*. There are several cases of deficient rhyme and metrical oversights, an Alexandrine being twice left in the middle of a stanza, while the Alexandrine is itself sometimes supplanted by a line of five or seven feet; the language also is, in places, involved and obscure. But with all its artistic defects *Laon and Cythna* can never lose its hold on the affection of those readers who sympathise with the spirit of the poem.

The relationship of Laon and Cythna in the original edition was intended not to condone incest, but "to startle the reader from the trance of ordinary life." This subject is several times introduced by Shelley in all frankness and simplicity, first during the Marlow period in *Laon and Cythna* and several passages of *Rosalind and Helen*, and later still in parts of *Epipsychidion*, and a letter of 1819. When *Laon and Cythna* was altered to *The Revolt of Islam*, Shelley protested that the poem was spoiled. The true text and title have now been restored in Mr. Forman's edition.

(4.) *Prince Athanase*, a fragment in *terza rima*, was

written at Marlow in 1817, probably late in the year. In 1820 Shelley meditated publishing it in a volume with *Julian and Maddalo* and other poems, but this was not done, and it first appeared in the *Posthumous Poems* in 1824. In the first sketch the title was *Pandemos and Urania*.

Summary.—Part I. describes the character of Prince Athanase, the grey-haired youth, who bears a close resemblance to the Poet in *Alastor*, Laon in *Laon and Cythna*, and Lionel in *Rosalind and Helen*, and is evidently an autobiographical sketch. The first and second fragments of *Part II.* narrate the friendship of Athanase and Zonoras, the "divine old man," who, like the Hermit in *Laon and Cythna*, was intended for Dr. Lind. In the third fragment Prince Athanase sets forth on his travels, and in the fourth the subject of love is commenced.

From Mrs. Shelley's note it appears that the main subject of the complete poem would have been Prince Athanase's search after the Uranian Venus, the ideal love, and his meeting with Pandemos, the earthly Venus, who disappoints and deserts him. The poem would thus have borne a close resemblance to *Alastor* and *Epipsychidion*, *q.v.* It was abandoned by Shelley as being morbid and over-refined, but his intention of publishing it three years later shows that he held it in some estimation. It was his first attempt in *terza rima*, and in skilful handling of that metre is only inferior to *The Triumph of Life*.

(5.) *Rosalind and Helen, a Modern Eclogue*, was begun at Marlow in 1817, whether before or after the writing of *Laon and Cythna* is uncertain, and finished at Mrs. Shelley's request at the Baths of Lucca in the summer of 1818. It was published in a volume with three other poems in the spring of 1819 (*vide* p. 119). There is a prefatory "Advertisement" by Shelley in which he defines the scope of the poem. The metre is chiefly the *iambic tetrameter*, popularised by Scott and Byron, but varying and irregular, some lines having no corresponding rhymes.

Summary.—The scene is laid at the Lake of Como, where Helen with her child meets Rosalind, who had renounced her friendship on account of her connection with Lionel. They now become reconciled, and sitting on a stone seat beside a spring in the forest they compare the stories of their lives. Rosalind first relates how she had been betrothed to a youth who, at the very altar, was found to be her half-brother. He died; and she was then married to a tyrant husband, after whose death, her children, by his will, were taken from her charge. Helen's story is devoted to a description of the character of her lover, Lionel; her love for him; his imprisonment, release, and death. In the conclusion of the poem we learn that Rosalind and Helen henceforth live together in Helen's house; Rosalind's daughter is restored to her, and afterwards betrothed to Helen's son. Helen outlives Rosalind.

The story of *Rosalind and Helen* was probably suggested by Mary Shelley's early friendship with Isabel Baxter having been broken off on account of her connection with Shelley. It is called a *Modern Eclogue* because it attempts to treat of real life, like the domestic idyll, the social degradation of women being the principal theme. It contains fine passages, but is on the whole the least successful of the longer poems. Shelley himself remarks that he laid "no stress on it," and that it was "not an attempt in the highest style of poetry." The narrative is certainly weak and disjointed, and leaves no strong impression on the mind.

(6.) *Julian and Maddalo, a Conversation*, was written at Este in the autumn of 1818, and sent to England for publication, but for some reason Leigh Hunt kept it back, and it first appeared in *Posthumous Poems*, 1824. In August 1818, Shelley visited Byron at Venice, and rode with him every evening; this was the origin of *Julian and Maddalo*, which Shelley wrote in a summer-house at I Capuccini, Byron's villa at Este, among the Euganean Hills, about thirty miles from Venice. The two chief characters of the

"Conversation" are Count Maddalo (Byron) and Julian (Shelley, doubtless with reference to the Emperor Julian, "the apostate"), while the Maniac, a mysterious person of whom Shelley affects in his Preface to know nothing, is probably, as is hinted in a letter to Leigh Hunt, another portrait of himself, "but with respect to time and place, ideal."

Summary.—Julian relates a conversation held with Maddalo as they rode along the Lido (with this part of the poem compare the letter to Mrs. Shelley of August 23, 1818, where the Lido is described as "a long sandy island, which defends Venice from the Adriatic"). To gain a better view of the sunset they embark in the Count's gondola, in which they pass a madhouse where a bell was tolling for vespers. (There is a doubt whether Shelley referred to the madhouse of San Servola, or to a building on the isle of San Clemente, now a penitentiary.) Next day Julian calls on Maddalo and sees his daughter, a fair and lovely child. (Allegra, daughter of Byron and Claire Clairmont, born in 1817.) They again go to the island, to see the maniac whom Maddalo had befriended. They are led to his chamber in the madhouse, where they overhear him as he talks to himself. The Maniac's soliloquy which follows has been rendered almost unintelligible for want of the full story of Shelley's life. It is partly autobiographical, partly ideal; the story of his unhappy marriage with Harriet being merged in the account of the fruitless search after the Uranian Venus (vide *Alastor* and *Epipsychidion*). Julian and Maddalo then leave him, and years later, Julian returning to Venice, hears further news of him from Maddalo's daughter, now grown to womanhood. He refuses, however, to communicate what he learnt to "the cold world." (This of course was a purely imaginary anticipation. Shelley never revisited Venice; and Allegra died in 1822.)

In *Julian and Maddalo* Shelley shows a firmer grasp of his subject than in any previous poem, and uses the heroic metre, as in the *Letter to Maria Gisborne*, in a familiar and yet thoroughly poetical manner which was altogether his own. *Julian and Maddalo* has sometimes been instanced together with *The Cenci* as an objective poem, but it is in reality highly subjective, presenting us at once with a sketch of Shelley's character at the time, and an episode of his past life. The obscurity of the personal allusions in the latter part of the poem, like those in *Epipsychidion*, is its chief blemish. For his relations with Byron, *vide* p. 22.

(7.) *Lines written among the Euganean Hills.* This poem was written at Este in October 1818, after an excursion among the Euganean Hills, on the southern slopes of which Este lies. It was published in the *Rosalind and Helen* volume early in 1819. Shelley here first uses the seven-syllabled trochaic metre, which afterwards became a favourite with him.

Summary.—The opening lines strike a note of deep despondency (vide "Advertisement" prefixed to *Rosalind and Helen*). Life is a sea of misery, made tolerable to the mariner only by occasional flowery islands, intervals of rest and comfort, such as the day the poet had just spent among the Euganean Hills. He describes the sunrise he had there witnessed, and the view of distant Venice. This leads him to moralise on the departed greatness of Venice, and her present slavery under the yoke of Austria, the "Celtic Anarch;" and to refer to Byron, who had there found a refuge. Then, as the sun rises higher, he looks down on Padua, once the seat of learning, now enslaved by the "Celts"; there is also a reference to the death of Ezzelin (tyrant of Padua in the thirteenth century; mentioned by Dante, *Inferno*, xii. 110). Noon and evening are in turn described; and with evening sorrowful remembrances come back. The island of rest is now to be left behind; the pilot, Pain, again sits at the helm; but the poet is comforted by the hope of touching at similar resting-places in his future voyage through life, and concludes with a prophetic vision of one such perfect island home.

Shelley is at his best in this mood and metre; the descriptions of the autumnal sunrise and noon, with the views of Venice and Padua, are among the finest in his writings. Mr. Swinburne has described this poem as "a rhapsody of thought and feeling, coloured by contact with nature, but not born of the contact." The same idea of a blissful isle of refuge is worked out more fully in *Epipsychidion* and its "Advertisement." In a letter to Mrs. Shelley in 1821, he talks of retiring with her and their child "to a solitary island in the sea." It is noticeable that in *Julian and Maddalo* the Euganean hills are described as resembling "a clump of peakéd isles," when seen from the Lido at Venice.

(8.) *Prometheus Unbound* was begun at Este in 1818, and the first three acts were completed at Rome in the spring of 1819. The fourth act, an afterthought, was written at Florence in December 1819. It was published about August 1820, with nine shorter poems (*vide* p. 119). *Prometheus Unbound* was in great part written among the ruined Baths of Caracalla, described in one of the letters to Peacock, scenery well suited to so lofty and solemn a theme. The subject is in the main the same as that of *Queen Mab* and *Laon and Cythna*—the struggle of humanity against its oppressors; but it is treated in a more ideal and less polemical manner. For the title and general form of the poem Shelley was indebted to Æschylus, who in his *Prometheus Bound* represented Prometheus ("forethought"), the champion of mankind, fettered by the tyrant Zeus; and also wrote a concluding drama now lost, in which Zeus and Prometheus were reconciled. Shelley, dismissing the idea of reconciliation, depicts the release and triumph of Prometheus, in other words, the emancipation of humanity. For Prometheus, in Shelley's poem, is the incarnation of the Human Mind; Asia, his consort, representing Nature, the spirit of immortal Love, and Jupiter being the embodiment of Tyranny and Custom. *Prometheus Unbound*, like *Hellas*,

is entitled a *lyrical* drama; the lyrics in fact are as prominent as the blank verse, and the lack of "dramatic
action" was intentional.

Summary.—In the Preface, Shelley touches on his debt
to Æschylus, his position with regard to his contemporaries,
and his "passion for reforming the world." *Act I.* Prometheus, chained to a precipice of the Indian Caucasus, solilo-
quises on his centuries of suffering, and converses with the
Earth, his mother. Mercury, Jove's herald (the spirit of
compromise), then brings the Furies (demons of doubt and
remorse) to torture Prometheus; who is comforted by the
two sisters of Asia, the nymphs Panthea and Ione (faith
and hope?), and by the songs of the spirits of the human
mind sent up by the Earth. *Act II.* describes the journey
of Asia with Panthea, who acts as the messenger of love
between Prometheus and his consort, from a lonely vale in
the Caucasus (scene i.), through forests and rocky heights
(scenes ii., iii.), to the cave of Demogorgon (Eternity; the
stern justice which awaits tyranny). There she inquires
when the time of liberation shall come, and sees the vision
of the Hours (scene iv.). Thence they ascend to a mountain
top where a voice is heard (that of Prometheus?) singing
the hymn of the genius of humanity to the spirit of nature,
to which Asia replies in another song. *Act III.* Jupiter,
exulting on his throne in heaven, is confronted by Demogorgon, who arrives in the Car of the Hour and summons
him to the abyss (scene i.). Apollo relates Jove's fall to
Neptune (scene ii.). Hercules unbinds Prometheus, who is
united to Asia. The "Spirit of the Hour" receives a
mystic shell, from which is to be breathed the trumpet-
blast of freedom. Then follow the speeches of the renovated
Earth (scene iii.); the Spirit of the Earth (distinct from the
Earth herself); and the Spirit of the Hour, who describes
how the fall of tyranny everywhere resulted from the sound
of the shell. (Here the poem ended in Shelley's first plan.)
Act IV. is chiefly lyrical, "the choral song of the regenerated

universe." Panthea and Ione listen to spirit songs, and then see a vision of the chariots of the moon (feminine grace), and the Spirit of the Earth (masculine energy), who sing to each other in alternate strains. The poem closes with the solemn words of Demogorgon.

Prometheus Unbound is Shelley's greatest and most characteristic work; he himself considered it his master-piece, though he foresaw that it could not be popular. The Myth, for such it is, is cast in a colossal mould, and resembles the mysterious conceptions of Blake; yet the meaning is clear enough in outline, if not in every detail. The principle that underlies it is that evil is accidental to man's nature and not inherent in it, and that the world may be regenerated by the power of love. Shelley thus put a new and deeper meaning into the framework of the old Greek legend. The first union of Prometheus and Asia, which is understood to have existed before Jove's. tyranny began, is the Saturnian Age of primitive innocence and natural simplicity; then follows the dominion of the usurper, when man is separated from nature; lastly, by the release of Prometheus, and his final union with Asia, is inaugurated the perfect age of mature wisdom and natural love. *Prometheus Unbound* is the poem of liberated humanity; the supreme expression of the great humanitarian movement of this century. It is for this reason that the conception of the Titan Prometheus is loftier than that of Milton's Satan, or any of the other titanic creations of poets and myth-writers. The character of Job is perhaps the one with which Prometheus may be most fitly compared.

The Italian influence is very perceptible in *Prometheus Unbound* in the calmer and stronger tone inspired by climate and surroundings. The mind is directed to the worship of ideal beauty, rather than to the denunciation of existing wrongs. There is a corresponding increase in poetical strength, the majestic melody of the blank verse being only surpassed by the sweetness of the lyrics, which reach their crowning excellence in the chorus at the end of *Act I.*, the two songs at the end of *Act II.*, and the spirit voices of *Act IV.* The hymn to the spirit of nature ("Life of Life") is the most impassioned of all Shelley's poems. The chief fault of *Prometheus Unbound* is that Shelley was occasionally led by his subtle metaphysical fancies to over-ingenious conceptions—as in the case of the "phantasm of Jupiter" in the opening act (comp. Mahmud's "Phantom" in *Hellas*), nor has he always succeeded in making the titanic dignity of the characters quite harmonise with their quasi-human relationship.

(9.) *The Sensitive Plant* was written at Pisa, in winter, early in 1820, and published with *Prometheus Unbound* the same year. The idea is said to have been suggested by the numerous flowers in Mrs. Shelley's drawing-room at Pisa; but we naturally recall to mind the account in Hogg's *Life of Shelley* (vol. i., p. 117) of Shelley and Hogg discovering a secluded flower-garden in one of their country rambles at Oxford, and Shelley's rhapsody about the imaginary Lady of the garden. In a letter of 1822, Shelley says that Jane Williams was "the exact antitype of the Lady," although the story was written before he knew her. The reference to flowers and plants during the residence at Pisa are numerous (cf. *The Question, The Zucca,* the gourd-boats of *The Witch of Atlas* (stanzas 32, 33), and *Fragments of an Unfinished Drama*). In a letter of January 1822, Shelley writes: "Our windows are full of plants which turn the sunny winter into spring."

Summary.—*Part I.* describes the garden in spring-time, the various flowers, and the Sensitive Plant, ever thirsting for absent love. *Part II.* gives the character of the Lady of the garden, her tender care of the flowers, and her death. *Part III.* The gradual decay of the neglected garden in autumn and winter; the death of the Sensitive Plant. In the "Conclusion" we find some striking speculations on death. Are the Sensitive Plant and the Lady in

E

reality dead? Or may not death itself be a mere illusion, love and beauty the only true reality?

The "companionless" Sensitive Plant, with its insatiable yearning for the ideal Beauty, is a type of the poet, in fact of Shelley himself (cf. *Alastor* and *Epipsychidion*). The concluding remarks about death are an instance of Shelley's leaning to the Berkeleyan philosophy, which regarded the material universe as only existing by a perception of the mind, the mind itself being eternal. There are many suggestions in Shelley's works of this unreality of death (comp. *Adonais*, "'Tis death is dead, not he," and *vide* p. 27).

(10.) *Letter to Maria Gisborne*, dated July 1, but probably written in June 1820, at Leghorn. Published in *Posthumous Poems*, 1824. The Gisbornes, who were absent on a journey to England, had lent their house to the Shelleys, and Shelley wrote the letter in the workshop of Henry Reveley, an engineer, son of Mrs. Gisborne by a former marriage. Maria Gisborne was a lady of keen and sensitive nature, once closely acquainted with Godwin and Mary Wollstonecraft, and now a cordial friend of the Shelleys. The letter is written in the poetic-familiar style of *Julian and Maddalo*, and is interesting as describing Shelley's way of life at Leghorn, and enumerating his friends in London. It should be compared with a prose letter to Mr. and Mrs. Gisborne written from Pisa on May 26th, 1820, in which Godwin, Hunt, and Hogg are also mentioned.

Summary.—Shelley describes Reveley's workshop, in which he was writing, overlaid with screws, cones, wheels, and blocks. On the table is a bowl of quicksilver, with mathematical instruments, bills, books, and all kinds of litter, lying about. He expresses hopes of renewed meetings with the Gisbornes, and reminiscences of old pleasures; and then proceeds to enumerate the friends they will see in London, viz., Godwin, Coleridge (*vide* p. 80, Shelley did not himself know Coleridge), Leigh Hunt, Hogg, Peacock, and Horace Smith (*vide* pp. 21, 22). He concludes by contrasting

London and Italy, and urges that they must pass next winter with him.

(11.) *The Witch of Atlas* was written in August 1820, at the Baths of San Giuliano, near Pisa, in the three days immediately following a solitary excursion to Monte San Pellegrino. It was sent to London, but not published till the *Posthumous Poems* appeared in 1824. The idea was probably suggested by the Homeric *Hymn to Mercury* which Shelley had just translated (*vide* p. 98), for the elfish nature of the Witch is very like that of Mercury, to whom indeed she is related by birth as well as character, both being grandchildren of Atlas. Both poems have the same metre, *ottava rima*, and are written in the same fantastic tone; there is also a striking resemblance between the opening passages. This subtle Mercurial character had doubtless a sympathetic attraction for Shelley, who used to be told by Leigh Hunt that "he had come from the planet Mercury" (cf. the remarks on the bowl of quicksilver, "that dew which the gnomes drink," in *Letter to Maria Gisborne*). But here again, as in the Myth of Prometheus, Shelley breathed a new spirit into the old Classical form. His "lady witch" is the incarnation of ideal beauty, and, like the fairy Mab, the patroness of free thought and free love among mankind. *The Witch of Atlas* is perhaps the most impalpable of all Shelley's poems, and by its very nature baffles criticism and explanation.

Summary.—In the Dedication *To Mary* Shelley playfully alludes to her being "critic-bitten," she having objected to his "visionary rhyme," because it lacked human interest. The opening stanzas describe the birth of the lady witch, and how she was visited by "all living things"—wild beasts, fawns, nymphs, Pan, Priapus, centaurs, satyrs, and shepherds. Then we read of her dwelling on Mount Atlas, with its stores of treasures, visions, odours, scrolls, chalices, and spices; her magic boat, scooped out of a gourd (comp. a similar idea in the *Fragments of an Unfinished Drama*);

her attendant creature, "Hermaphroditus;" her voyages to the "Austral lake," "Old Nilus," and cloud-land; her pranks and visits to mortals (comp. *Queen Mab*); lastly, her beneficence, especially to poets and lovers.

(12.) *Epipsychidion; Verses addressed to the noble and unfortunate Lady Emilia V——, now imprisoned in the Convent of ——*, was written at Pisa in 1821, probably early in the year, and published anonymously in 1821, for "the esoteric few" who were likely to appreciate it (*vide* p. 120). The meaning of the title is "a poem on the soul" (Psyche); the lady to whom this poem was addressed was Emilia Viviani, who was shut up by her father, an Italian count, in the convent of St. Anne, Pisa, where the Shelleys made her acquaintance and befriended her. The subject of *Epipsychidion*, which was inspired by the *Vita Nuova* of Dante, is the ideal love, here identified with Shelley's spiritual affection for Emilia; he also gives us "an idealised history" of his own life and feelings. The poem is attributed in the "Advertisement" to a writer who died at Florence.

Summary.—*Epipsychidion* begins with an invocation of Emilia, which rises higher and higher in successive gradations of passionate appeal. In a famous passage, which recalls *Queen Mab* and its *Notes*, the difference between true love and the matrimonial bondage is insisted on. Then the poet relates his own career; how in his search for the ideal, he found in her stead the earthly love, "one whose voice was venomed agony." (His first marriage is probably alluded to.) While he rashly sought "the shadow" in many mortal forms (the personal allusions are here too obscure for satisfactory explanation), deliverance at last shines on him in a moon-like shape (Mary Godwin), the reflection of the true ideal light. After more storms, the vision of the Sun (Emilia) rises on him, in which he recognises the real object of his search. Henceforth he will live under the alternate empire of Sun and Moon. Finally, he summons Emilia to sail with him to an Ionian isle, which is described at some length (comp. the closing passage of *Lines written among the Eugancan Hills*). At the end of *Epipsychidion* are subjoined thirteen lines in which the poet bids his verses go forth to the initiated few who will appreciate them. Among these are " Marina " (Mrs. Shelley), " Vanna " (diminutive for Giovanna, Jane Williams), and " Primus " (Edward Williams ?).

In *Epipsychidion* we have Shelley's fullest, though not most consistent, development of his doctrine of love, based on Plato's *Symposium* and Dante's *Vita Nuova*. In this respect *Epipsychidion* is closely akin to *Alastor*, *Hymn to Intellectual Beauty*, and *Prince Athanase ;* though it should be noticed that in identifying Emilia with the spirit of love, he was confusing the actual with the ideal, and so transgressing his own Platonic doctrine as stated in *The Zucca*. In the autobiographical passages of *Epipsychidion* there is much resemblance to the story of the Maniac in *Julian and Maddalo*, the obscurity of the personal allusions being the chief poetical flaw in both cases. *Epipsychidion* has always been the despair of the critics ; it is a rhapsody which only the sympathetic will understand, and Shelley was well aware of this himself, as appears from his " Advertisement," the instructions sent to his publisher, and letters to friends. As regards the beauty of the heroic verse in which *Epipsychidion* is written, there can be little difference of opinion ; to find anything comparable to it, we must go back to Marlowe's *Hero and Leander*.

The fullest account of Emilia Viviani is that given by Medwin (*Life of Shelley*, vol. ii.), and quoted in the appendix to Forman's edition. Emilia is stated to have been married to a husband whom she did not love, and to have died six years later ; but there is some reason for doubting Medwin's correctness on the latter point. Shelley's lines *To E—— V——* (1821) should be read with *Epipsychidion ; vide* also *Fiordispina*. There are some interesting fragments and cancelled passages of *Epipsychidion*.

(13.) *Adonais, an Elegy on the Death of John Keats,* was written and printed at Pisa about June 1821, copies being sent to London for publication the same year (*vide* p. 120). Keats, of whom Shelley was a friend and correspondent, had died at Rome, February 23, 1821, and Shelley, as his Preface shows, shared the common but erroneous belief that his death was caused by the savage criticism of the *Quarterly Review.* The name Adonais, here given to Keats, was doubtless suggested by Bion's dirge for Adonis, of which Adonais is the Doric form.

Summary.—The Muse, Urania, is bidden lament for Adonais, her youngest poet, as she wept before for Milton, now "the third among the sons of light." (Homer and Dante are probably alluded to as the first and second, vide *A Defence of Poetry,* p. 110.) The dreams and fancies of Adonais are pictured as mourning round his body, while nature itself weeps in sympathy. Urania speeds to the death-chamber, and utters her lamentation ; then come the "mountain shepherds," the "pilgrim of eternity" (Byron), Ierne's lyrist (Moore), the frail Form, "a phantom among men" (Shelley), and the "gentlest of the wise" (probably Leigh Hunt). The poet, after briefly lashing the anonymous writer of the review, then turns to the subject of immortality. Adonais is not dead, but absorbed into the loveliness of nature ; for the world's luminaries, such as Chatterton, Sidney, Lucan, may be eclipsed, but cannot be extinguished. Rome, where Adonais lies, is the subject of the concluding stanzas ; the English burying-place under the pyramid of Cestius is alluded to (comp. the prose description in the letter to Peacock from Naples, December 22, 1818), and by a strange prescience Shelley speaks of himself as about to follow Adonais.

In *Adonais* Shelley again makes use of a classical model ; this time taking as a framework the style of those Greek idyllic writers, whose poetry he describes in his *Defence of Poetry* as "intensely melodious," though "with an excess of sweetness." His intimacy with Bion and Moschus is shown by some of his translations (*vide* p. 99). In the first part of the poem this classical influence is as clearly traced as in Milton's *Lycidas*, to which *Adonais* has many points of resemblance ; but Shelley is more successful in avoiding the confusion of ancient with modern ideas; there are no fauns and satyrs in his elegy, but all is transformed by modern thought and poetical mysticism. In the second part he breaks away from his originals, to treat of the subject of death and immortality, his utterances in *Adonais* being the most positive indications he gives of a belief in a future life (*vide* p. 27). The personal forebodings of death in the last stanzas are one of those strange occurrences of which there are several instances in Shelley's life (*vide* p. 16). His friend-ship and admiration for Keats, though very cordial and sincere, as is shown by several of his letters, especially that to the editor of the *Quarterly Review* (1820), would hardly of themselves have made him long to rejoin his lost friend; but it must be remembered that his feelings towards Keats are idealised in *Adonais,* as was his love for Emilia in *Epi-psychidion.* As regards style and workmanship, *Adonais* is generally considered, as Shelley himself believed it, the most perfect of his longer poems. The Spenserian metre is used with more finish and mastery than in *Laon and Cythna;* but through his adhesion to a classical model, we perhaps miss some of the charm of his wild originality and lyric rapture.

(14.) *Hellas, a Lyrical Drama*, written at Pisa in the autumn of 1821, and published early the next year (*vide* p. 120), was the last poem given to the world in Shelley's lifetime. It is a tribute to the Greek nation, inspired by the enthu-siasm Shelley felt on hearing of the proclamation of Greek independence (1821), and in its general form is based on the *Persæ* of Æschylus, which was a triumph-song over the defeat of the Persians at Salamis. *Hellas*, which describes in sanguine anticipation the fall of the Moslem empire and the freedom of Greece (a vision realised in part by the battle of Navarino, 1827), is lyrical rather than dramatic, and cannot be classed with precision with any of the other poems, being, as Shelley himself wrote of it, "a sort of lyrical, dramatic, nondescript piece of business." Though professing to deal with contemporary events, it is, in the main, ideal, being a poetic description of the world's passion for liberty; herein resembling *Laon and Cythna*, and the more so since in both poems the scene is laid in the "Golden City" and the Levant. The Dedication to Prince Mavrocordato, who first brought Shelley the news of the insurrection, is dated November 1, 1821. In his Preface, Shelley insists on the world's debt to Greece, and points out the true policy of England. The title *Hellas* was suggested by Edward Williams.

Summary.—The scene is Constantinople. A chorus of Greek captives sing of the hopes of freedom, while the Sultan (Mahmud II., who reigned 1808–1839) sleeps and dreams of danger. He wakes in sudden alarm, and learns from Hassan of a Jew, Ahasuerus (*vide* p. 42), a wizard and interpreter of dreams, who has been summoned for consultation. Presently Daood brings news that the Janizaries are in revolt, and to satisfy their demand the Sultan is compelled to devote the treasures of Solyman. He is represented throughout as foreseeing the ruin of his empire, and his conversation with Hassan is so contrived as to emphasize this foreboding. Then messengers arrive in succession with news of repeated disasters. Lastly Ahasuerus enables Mahmud to see visions of the past, and also to divine the impending ruin by raising his own "imperial shadow" from the phantom-world (comp. the "Phantasm of Jupiter," in *Prometheus Unbound*).

Of the sublime choric songs with which *Hellas* is interspersed three are especially noteworthy, viz., those commencing "In the great morning of the world," "Worlds on worlds are rolling ever," and the concluding chorus "The world's great age begins anew," which may be compared with Byron's *Isles of Greece*. The second illustrates Shelley's attitude towards Christianity, a subject treated more fully in his *Notes to Hellas*. As in *The Cenci* he represents religion not from his own standpoint but from that of a Catholic country, so in *Hellas* he recognises the fact that Christianity compared with other religions may possess a relative if not an absolute truth (*vide* p. 28). In a striking fragment, entitled *Prologue to Hellas*, probably part of an earlier sketch (Forman's edition, iv. 94), Christ, Satan, and Mahomet are represented as contending before the throne of God for the possession of Greece, Christ being the champion of liberty and civilisation.

(15.) *The Triumph of Life* was written at Lerici on the Gulf of Spezzia in the spring and early summer of 1822 and published in *Posthumous Poems*, 1824. It was the last of Shelley's great works, a fragment in *terza rima*. The subject, as indicated by the title, is the triumphal procession of the powers of Life, dragging captive the spirit of Man; but we can only guess at what the full poem would have been from the majestic proportions of the fragment. It was composed by Shelley as he sailed along the Italian coast in his yacht, the "Ariel," under the blaze of the summer sun, or as he sat floating in a little "shallop" on the moonlit waves; and these influences have left a strong mark on the rhythm and imagery. Dante and Petrarch are the poets to whom Shelley was here most indebted.

Summary.—The opening of the poem is similar in form to that of *Laon and Cythna*, *Ode to Liberty*, and *Ode to Naples*, and describes a trance that fell on the poet at sunrise (the sun is possibly meant to be a type of the ideal, as the moon of actual life, cf. *Epipsychidion*). The vision is then described. The poet sees an onward-streaming multitude accompanying a moon-like chariot in which sits a gloomy shape (Life; the actual, as opposed to the spiritual). The chariot is driven by a "Janus-visaged shadow" (Destiny; ·

or human reason (?)), while round and behind it troop the captive multitudes. A voice from the wayside proves to be that of Rousseau, who appears in strangely distorted shape, and his conversation with Shelley continues to the end of the fragment. He points out other captives, Napoleon, Voltaire, Plato, "the tutor and his pupil" (Aristotle and Alexander), Bacon, and a company of other great men. His own story is then given ; which resembles parts of *Epipsychidion* and *Julian and Maddalo.* He relates how he awoke to "the young year's dawn," and how a temptress, "a shape all light," gave him the cup which betrayed him from the ideal to the actual, and made him a victim of life's pageant. The fragment ends with Shelley's question, "Then what is Life ? "

The *Triumph of Life* may be compared with Tennyson's *Vision of Sin.* That, so far as it goes, it was written in no hopeful tone is clear from even Plato being classed among the misguided captives ; but it is possible that the poem, if completed, would have dealt with the liberating power of Love. As it stands there is much in it that is mysterious and obscure. The long line and mazy dance of the visionary multitude is wonderfully expressed in the continuous rhythm of the *terza rima.*

II. Dramas.

(1.) *The Cenci* was begun at Rome, May 14, 1819, the dedication to Leigh Hunt being dated May 29; but it was not finished till about the middle of August, the greater part being written at Leghorn in a small roofed terrace at the top of the Villa Valsovano. It was printed at Leghorn in 1819, and published in England in the spring of 1820; a second edition followed in 1821, a proof of popularity which none of Shelley's other poems achieved. It was Shelley's desire that *The Cenci* should be acted at Covent Garden, with Miss O'Neil as Beatrice ; but this was declined by the manager of the theatre on account of the nature of the play. Shelley derived the material of the tragedy from an old manuscript which came into his hands in Italy; his enthusiasm was roused by Guido's picture of Beatrice and the national interest which the story had excited; and he was thus induced by Mrs. Shelley to write a drama on the subject, in spite of his deficiency, real or fancied, in dramatic talent. His remarks on the manuscript account, which he wished to prefix to his play, and the proper method of treating it dramatically, may be seen in his Preface. The actual date of the events alluded to was 1599, in the Pontificate of Clement VIII.; but the latest historical investigations tend to take away much of the romantic element of the story.

The interest of *The Cenci* centres almost exclusively on the two chief characters, which it happened were such as Shelley was well qualified to draw. Count Cenci is the embodiment of a long life spent in tyranny and crime, which have been fostered by success till they amount almost to madness. His cruel and restless spirit still craves new victims on whom to wreak its fury; hence he conceives the idea of inflicting a crowning outrage on his daughter Beatrice, while co-existing with this diabolic wickedness is a firm faith in religion, and a superstitious disposition to see in everything the direct agency of God's providence. The character of Beatrice is a mixture of womanly gentleness and unfaltering courage; the crimes and miseries with which the circumstances of her life have encircled her are quite external to her true nature. She errs in seeking revenge for the wrong her father inflicts on her; but it is precisely in this error that the dramatic interest of her position consists. The weakness of the other characters, whether intentional or not on Shelley's part, serves to throw those of Count Cenci and Beatrice into stronger relief; though it is to be regretted that Orsino, the crafty priest, was not more powerfully delineated.

Summary.—The play falls naturally into two parts, Count

Cenci being the prominent charactèr in the first, Beatrice in the second. The first three acts, in which the scene is laid at Rome, exhibit Cenci at the height of his monstrous career of wickedness, now rapidly approaching its close. In the banquet scene (act i. sc. 3) we see him exulting over the death of his sons, and then planning worse outrage against his daughter. This drives his family in desperation to devise the plot against his life, in which they are aided by the double-dealing Orsino, who himself has crafty designs on Beatrice. The fourth act opens at the Castle of Petrella, Cenci's stronghold in the Apulian Apennines ; but after the first scene, which describes his summons to Beatrice, and the curse pronounced on her when she refuses to obey, Cenci does not again appear on the stage, and our whole attention is henceforth riveted on Beatrice. The murder scene is immediately followed by the arrival of the Pope's Legate with a warrant for Cenci's death ; but that just punishment has been anticipated by the lawless vengeance of his family, on whom suspicion at once falls. The last act, where the scene is again at Rome, is occupied with Beatrice's splendid though paradoxical denial of the charge of parricide. Her intrepid spirit rises higher and higher, as the toils close around her in hall of justice and prison cell, while her tenderness and gentle pity for her mother and brother are equally conspicuous. As the darkness of hatred and horror broods over the earlier parts of *The Cenci*, so the closing scenes are illuminated by the glory of love.

Shelley's chief deviation from the manuscript account consists in making the detection of Count Cenci's murder follow immediately on the crime, instead of six months later ; he also touches more lightly and delicately on the darker details of the story. The *Œdipus Tyrannus* of Sophocles was doubtless in his mind when dealing with a subject so full of horror ; there are also many passages suggestive of the influence of Ford and Webster, the determination of Beatrice not to confess the murder resembling that of Vittoria Corombona in *The White Devil.* Unconscious plagiarisms from Shakspere are numerous in *The Cenci* (*vide* p. 45); the most obvious being that from Macbeth in the murder scene. In spite of these obligations *The Cenci* is by far the grandest and most original English drama produced since the Elizabethan period. In this poem Shelley deliberately curtailed the profusion of poetical imagery with which his lyrics abound; the blank verse is direct and concentrated, and there can be no possible suggestion of a 'lack of human interest.' It has remained for the Shelley Society to carry out the wish of the poet by the performance of *The Cenci*, May 7, 1886, sixty-seven years after it was written. The subject of the Cenci trial is treated of in Landor's *Five Scenes*, and alluded to in Browning's *Cenciaja.* Count Cenci's character has been compared with that of Guido Franceschini in *The Ring and the Book.*

(2.) *Charles the First*, a fragment, was written in the winter of 1821–22, at Pisa. Part of it was published in the *Posthumous Poems*, 1824, and the rest added by Mr. Rossetti in his edition of 1870. Shelley had for some time meditated a drama on this subject; but when he began to write it his progress was slow, and he finally abandoned it in favour of *The Triumph of Life*, his dislike of history being probably the chief cause of the failure. Yet, as far as it goes, *Charles the First* is a striking and powerful attempt. In scene i. the murmuring of the discontented citizens as they watch the Queen's masque passing through the streets forebodes the troubles that are to come. Scene ii. shows us the King, amiable by nature, but the slave of circumstances, urged into tyrannous courses by the ambition of the Queen, the bigotry of Laud, and the cunning of Strafford. Archy, the Fool (an imitation of the Fool in *King Lear*), is alone wise enough to foresee the gathering storm. The three remaining scenes are quite fragmentary, but Hampden's tribute to America (scene iv.) and Archy's song (" A Widow-bird," scene 5) are specially noteworthy. Shelley speaks severely of the character of

Charles in his *Philosophical View of Reform*, but he was careful to repress his party spirit in the drama.

(3.) *Fragments of an Unfinished Drama*, written at Pisa, probably in the spring of 1822. The opening portions were published in the *Posthumous Poems*, 1824, and the rest added in Garnett's *Relics of Shelley*, 1862 (under the title of *The Magic Plant*), and Rossetti's edition of 1870. The intended plot of the fragment, which was written to amuse Shelley's circle of friends at Pisa, is explained in Mrs. Shelley's *Notes*. In the first short fragment an enchantress living in an isle of the Indian Archipelago laments the departure of a Pirate, whose life she had saved ; and summons a Spirit for the purpose of luring him back to her. The Spirit's speech is the most striking instance of unconscious 'plagiarism in all Shelley's writings, being almost a reproduction of the opening lines of Milton's *Comus*. The second fragment is a conversation between an Indian Youth and a Lady. The Lady is in quest of her lover, the Pirate, and has met the Indian Youth on the island, his love for her being returned by sympathy and the affection of a sister. She tells him how she was brought to the island by a " magic plant " (comp. *Witch of Atlas*, 32, 33, and *The Zucca*, and *vide* p. 65). These fragments are rather a playful effort of the fancy than a serious dramatic attempt. Trelawny is evidently alluded to in the Pirate " of savage but noble nature ; " while Shelley and Jane Williams are perhaps the originals of the Youth and the Lady. There is an entry in Edward Williams' Diary for April 10, 1822, which seems to refer to the composition of this fragment.

The *Scene from Tasso* (*Relics of Shelley*, 1862) and *Song for Tasso* (*Posthumous Poems*, 1824) were written in 1818, when Shelley was meditating a tragedy on the subject of Tasso's madness, a plan which was perhaps given up on the appearance of Byron's *Lament of Tasso*. Another of Shelley's schemes was a drama founded on the Book of Job, but no traces exist of any attempt at this. The so-called *Prologue to Hellas* (*vide* p. 73) is a magnificent dramatic fragment, first published in *Relics of Shelley*, 1862. As regards Shelley's dramatic powers, *vide* p. 38.

III. Shorter Poems. Lyrics, Odes, Songs, &c., in Chronological Order.

Original Poetry, by Victor and Cazire, was published, 1810, by Stockdale, but withdrawn on his discovering that some of the poetry was *not* original. It was a joint composition ; Shelley being "Victor," with Harriet Grove, or Shelley's sister Elizabeth, or his friend Graham, as " Cazire." The poem is now missing.

Posthumous Fragments of Margaret Nicholson, published at Oxford in 1810, was a semi-burlesque volume in which Hogg had some part, the poems being attributed to a mad washerwoman who had attempted the life of George III. According to Hogg's account the hoax was successful, and the book had some circulation at Oxford, but the truth of this cannot be relied on.

The Wandering Jew, written, according to Medwin, about 1811, dealt at considerable length with a subject which made a great impression on Shelley's mind (*vide* p. 42). It was not published by Shelley, but four cantos appeared in *Fraser's Magazine*, July 1831, which Medwin asserted to be only a portion of the poem, viz., that which he himself had contributed to a joint composition. It was therefore supposed that Shelley's portion had been lost; but it is now thought probable that the poem was complete in the four cantos, and that Medwin's share in the writing was very small. (Cf. new edition of *The Wandering Jew*, with Notes by B. Dobell. Shelley Society's Publications.)

1812–1815.—*The Devil's Walk*, printed and distributed by Shelley in 1812, was founded on the poem by Southey and Coleridge of the same title. It was distributed, together with the *Declaration of Rights*, by Shelley's servant, Daniel Hill, who was for that reason arrested at Barnstaple in August 1812.

Stanzas, April 1814, published with *Alastor*, 1816.

("Away! the moor is dark beneath the moon.") These lines were written in reference to Shelley's leaving Mrs. Boinville's house at Bracknell to return to his unhappy life with Harriet.

To Mary Wollstonecraft Godwin ("Mine eyes were dim"), written June 1814, and published in *Posthumous Poems.* Previous to Rossetti's edition, 1870, this poem was wrongly dated 1821, under the title *To* ——. In reality it is an expression of Shelley's feelings a few weeks before his separation from Harriet.

To —— ("Oh there are spirits in the air"), published with *Alastor*, 1816, with a quotation prefixed from Euripides (*Hippolytus*, 1143). The lines are addressed to Coleridge, whose change of opinions and consequent unhappiness are deplored. Shelley did not know Coleridge personally, but alludes to him in the *Letter to Maria Gisborne*, and *Peter Bell*, part 5, stanzas 1–5.

A Summer-Evening Churchyard, Lechdale, Gloucestershire. These lines, which are pervaded by the melancholy tone common to all the poems published with *Alastor*, 1816, were written during Shelley's boating excursion to visit the source of the Thames, in the autumn of 1815.

Mutability. Published with *Alastor*, 1816. There is another poem of the same title, written in 1821. Shelley's mobile and changeful temperament made him an apt disciple of the doctrine of Heraclitus, viz., that "restless movement is the ultimate fact which meets us in every part of the universe. Such knowledge as shifting senses give of shifting particulars is not knowledge, but if all things are mutable, there is a law of mutability which is itself immutable." Compare his treatment of *The Cloud*, which changes but cannot die.

To Wordsworth. A sonnet, published with *Alastor*. Shelley, in spite of his admiration for Wordsworth's poetry, regarded him as "a lost leader." "That such a man should be such a poet!" he wrote in a letter to Peacock in July,

1818. (Compare also a reference to Wordsworth in the *Remarks on "Mandeville."*) In *Peter Bell* (*vide* p. 93) Shelley gave full vent to his indignation. This sonnet bears a striking resemblance to one translated by Shelley from the Italian in 1815 (*Guido Cavalcante to Dante*, vide p. 99).

1816.—*Hymn to Intellectual Beauty*, written in Switzerland in the summer of 1816; first published in the *Examiner* in January 1817; and included in the *Rosalind and Helen* volume, 1819. The idea of the poem, which in some ways resembles Wordsworth's ode on *Intimations of Immortality*, was conceived during Shelley's excursion with Byron on the Lake of Geneva, when his mind was full of Rousseau. The Spirit of Beauty to which Shelley appeals, the "unseen Power," whose visits to mortals are represented as inconstant and intermittent, is identical with the ideal Love of which Asia is the personification in *Prometheus Unbound* (*vide* also *Alastor* and *Epipsychidion*). Stanzas 5 and 6 should be read in connection with stanzas 3–5 of the Dedication of *Laon and Cythna*, as they refer to the same intellectual awakening at Sion House or Eton. There is also an allusion to this event in *Julian and Maddalo*, 380–382.

Mont Blanc, Lines written in the Vale of Chamouni, dated June 23, 1816, published in 1817 with the *History of a Six Weeks' Tour* (*vide* p. 119), and reprinted with *Posthumous Poems*. It was inspired by the view from the Bridge of Arve, and, as Shelley tells us in his Preface to the *Six Weeks' Tour*, is "an attempt to imitate the untameable wildness" of the scenes among which it was written. Mont Blanc is regarded as typical of the power and majesty of nature; while in the first and last stanzas we see traces of Shelley's Berkeleyan philosophy; even the Alps cannot exist independently of human thought.

1817.—*Marianne's Dream*, written at Marlow, 1817, and first published in Leigh Hunt's *Literary Pocket Book* for 1819; then with *Posthumous Poems*. Marianne was the

F

name of Mrs. Leigh Hunt, who related to Shelley the dream here described.

To William Shelley. These lines, published by Mrs. Shelley in 1839, were written in 1817, after the decision of the Chancery suit, under the idea that an attempt would be made to take away all Shelley's children. William, his eldest son by the second marriage, was born January 24, 1816. Comp. the two fragments written after his death (p. 84). The fourth stanza of this poem reappears in *Rosalind and Helen.*

To Constantia, Singing, published in *Posthumous Poems,* 1824. The lines were probably meant for Miss Clairmont. The name Constantia was that of the heroine of a novel, *Ormond,* which Shelley admired. There is a fragment *To Constantia,* also written in 1817.

Ozymandias, the finest of Shelley's sonnets, was published with *Rosalind and Helen,* 1819, and has been wrongly supposed to be the one written by Shelley in competition with Keats and Leigh Hunt. The sonnet-laws are here violated by the rhymes of the octave and sextell being interwoven. Ozymandias, or Rameses II., the Pharaoh of the oppression, reigned over Egypt about B.C. 1322, and is supposed to be the Sesostris of Greek legend. The fragments of his colossal statue lie near Thebes, with the inscription, " I am Ozymandias, king of kings. If you would know how great I am, and where I lie, surpass my works."

Lines to a Critic, published in *The Liberal,* 1823, and *Posthumous Poems,* 1824, should be compared with *Lines to a Reviewer,* 1820, as illustrative of Shelley's quiet and tolerant attitude towards hostile criticism. In a letter of 1822 he wrote, " The man must be enviably happy whom reviews can make miserable. I have neither curiosity, interest, pain, nor pleasure in anything, good or evil, they can say of me."

Lines (" That time is dead for ever, child ") dated by Mrs. Shelley, November 5, 1817. Harriet's suicide, which seems to be referred to, took place about November 9, 1816.

On F. G., written 1817, published in edition of 1839. Fanny Godwin, Mary Godwin's half-sister, committed suicide October 9, 1816.

1818.—*Sonnet to the Nile,* written early in 1818, before Shelley left England, and first published among Shelley's works in Forman's edition, 1877. This, and not *Ozymandias,* was probably the sonnet written in friendly competition with Keats and Leigh Hunt. It is as distinctly the least successful of the three as Hunt's is the best.

The Woodman and the Nightingale, a fragmentary poem, in *terza rima;* written at Naples in the winter of 1818; published in *Posthumous Poems* in 1824. The nightingale is the type of love; the rough woodman represents the hard hearts who expel it.

Marenghi (*Mazenghi* in edition of 1839) was written at Naples, December 1818. Some of it appeared in *Posthumous Poems,* 1824; the rest was added in Rossetti's edition, 1870. It is a fragment of a narrative poem in six-line stanzas, describing the conquest of Pisa by Florence, and the exploits of Marenghi, an exiled Florentine. The materials are drawn from Sismondi's *Histoire des Républiques Italiennes.*

Stanzas, written in dejection, near Naples, published in *Posthumous Poems,* 1824, dated December, 1818. The winter spent by Shelley at Naples, a time of depression and ill-health, left its mark on the poems then written—the despondent tone of which recalls that of *Alastor.* Medwin asserts that Shelley's dejection was caused by the death of the mysterious lady who was said to have followed him to Naples.

Song on a Faded Violet, published in *Posthumous Poems,* 1824, and classed by Mrs. Shelley with poems of 1818.

Sonnet ("Lift not the painted veil") published in *Posthumous Poems,* 1824, is interesting as containing a sketch of Shelley's own character, and his yearning after the spirit of love. It should be compared with the prose fragment *On Love.* In this so-called sonnet the sextell is found to precede the octave instead of following it.

Invocation to Misery was published in *The Athenæum,* 1832, *The Shelley Papers,* 1833, and under title of *Misery —a Fragment,* in the edition of 1839.

1819.—*The Indian Serenade,* first published in *The Liberal,* 1822. In the *Posthumous Poems* and edition of 1839 it was headed *Lines to an Indian Air,* and dated 1821. It has now been traced back at least to 1819, which disproves the tradition that Shelley first wrote the lines for an air brought from India by Jane Williams, though he doubtless rewrote them for her. Trelawny (i. 159) says Shelley spoke of having written the lines "long ago," and intended to improve them. There are several variations in the text.

To Sophia. These four stanzas, addressed by Shelley to Miss Sophia Stacey, who was a friend of the Shelleys in Italy, were first published in Rossetti's edition, 1870.

Love's Philosophy was published in *The Indicator* in December 1819. In *Posthumous Poems* it was wrongly dated 1820. It is inspired by Shelley's doctrine of universal love, and is apparently modelled on the form of an ode of Anacreon (xxi.) Whether Shelley was acquainted with the original Greek, or with the imitations by Ronsard and Cowley, is a matter of conjecture.

To William Shelley. There are two fragments with this title; one ("My lost William") written in June 1819, and published in *Posthumous Poems,* 1824; the other ("Thy little footsteps") first published in 1839. William Shelley died at Rome on June 7th, 1819, and was buried in the Protestant cemetery. He is referred to in *The Cenci,* act v. scene ii., in the account of Cardinal Camillo's nephew, "that fair blue-eyed child." *Vide* the lines *To William Shelley,* p. 82.

Ode to Heaven, published with *Prometheus Unbound,* 1820, is conceived in the lofty spirit of Shelley's Berkeleyan philosophy ; its subject is the immensity of creation.

An Exhortation, published with *Prometheus Unbound,*

1820. It is probably the "little thing about poets" which Shelley sent to Maria Gisborne, May 8th, 1820.

Ode to the West Wind was written in the autumn of 1819 in the Cascine, "a wood that skirts the Arno, near Florence" (*vide* Shelley's Note), and published with *Prometheus Unbound* in 1820. The leading idea of the poem is the sequence and balance of seasons (comp. the *Dirge for the Year* 1821, and *Laon and Cythna*, ix. 21); winter is at hand, yet spring cannot be far behind, a comforting thought which is applied in the last two stanzas to the genius of the poet himself. This ode, the most perfectly finished of all Shelley's lyrics, consists of five stanzas, each of fourteen lines, with the rhymes arranged after the fashion of the *terza rima* rather than the sonnet. The "foliage of the ocean," mentioned in the third stanza and the note thereon, is a favourite subject with Shelley, appearing again in *The Recollection, Ode to Naples, Ode to Liberty*, &c.

On the Medusa of Leonardo da Vinci, in the Florentine Gallery, written in the autumn of 1819, at Florence; published in *Posthumous Poems*, 1824. This poem, which was inspired by Shelley's studies in the picture galleries of Florence (*vide* p. 113), is full of intensely vivid descriptive power. Leigh Hunt wrote of it, "The poetry seems. sculptured and grinning, like the subject; the words are cut with a knife." In this respect it may be compared with *Ozymandias*.

For the chief lyrics in *Prometheus Unbound*, vide p. 65.

1820.—*Arethusa* is dated Pisa, 1820, and was probably written early in the year. It was published in *Posthumous Poems*, 1824. It is a poetical version of the Greek legend of the pursuit of the nymph Arethusa by the river god Alpheus. They start from Peloponnesus, and pass under the sea to their "Dorian home" in Sicily.

The Cloud, dated 1820 by Mrs. Shelley, was published with *Prometheus Unbound* the same year. Its metre is the same as that of *Arethusa*, which makes it probable that it was written at Pisa about the same time. Cloud scenery had at all times a great attraction for Shelley, and from his "tower window" at Leghorn he had special opportunities of watching it. Mrs. Shelley in her Preface speaks of Shelley "marking the cloud while he floated in his boat on the Thames," which has suggested the idea that this poem was written as early as 1818. The sixth stanza of *The Cloud* should be compared with a cancelled passage of *Epipsychidion* (Forman's Edition II., 393).

Ode to a Skylark, written at Leghorn in the summer of 1820, while the Shelleys were staying at the house of the Gisbornes, and published with *Prometheus Unbound* the same year. The idea was conceived during an evening walk among myrtle hedges, while the skylark was singing overhead. Here, as in the *Ode to the West Wind*, *The Sensitive Plant*, and many other poems, we note that strong personal element which led Shelley, like Wordsworth, to draw hope and comfort for man from the study of nature. Shelley's ode should be read with Wordsworth's poem *To a Skylark*, and Keats' *Ode to a Nightingale*.

Hymn of Apollo and *Hymn of Pan*, published in *Post-humous Poems*, were written at a friend's request to be inserted in a drama on the subject of *Midas*. Apollo and Pan are supposed to be contending for a prize.

The Question, published in *Posthumous Poems*, 1824. The title is explained by the concluding lines of the poem. It is written in *ottava rima*, which makes it probable that it dates from about the same time as the translation of Homer's *Hymn to Mercury* and *The Witch of Atlas*, *i.e.*, the summer of 1820. Shelley's love of flowers is here exemplified, as in other poems of his Pisan period (vide *The Sensitive Plant*, p. 65). It is noticeable that the last line of the first stanza has one redundant foot. The sixth line of stanza ii. ("Like a child, half in tenderness and mirth"), omitted in early editions, was restored by Dr. Garnett in 1870.

Ode to Liberty, written in the earlier half of 1820, and

published the same year with *Prometheus Unbound.* It was suggested by the insurrection in Spain in 1820, caused by the tyranny of Ferdinand VII. The ode is an idealised history of Liberty narrated to the poet by a spiritual "Voice out of the deep" (*vide* first and last stanzas), in the same way as the events in *Laon and Cythna*, the *Ode to Naples*, and *The Triumph of Life* are recorded as if seen in a vision. The progress of Liberty is traced after the first ages of chaos and tyranny (there is no mention here of a primeval golden age as in *Prometheus Unbound*, &c.), in the glories of Athens and Rome, which are ·succeeded by a thousand years of Christian oppression. At last the spirit of freedom is re-vived in the Renaissance, and again in the French Revolu-tion (stanzas 11, 12, where Napoleon is also alluded to). Then follows an appeal to England, Germany, and Italy. The free and wise are adjured to banish the names of King and Priest (*King* is the word concealed in early editions by the four asterisks in stanza 15; not *Christ*, as some have supposed), that Science and Art may be unfettered; but the true Liberty will ever be accompanied by Wisdom, Love, and Justice. The *Ode to Liberty*, in its stately rhythm, sublime imagery, and passionate worship of true freedom, as distinct from anarchy, is similar in many points to Coleridge's *Ode to France*, which Shelley greatly admired.

Liberty, a short poem of four stanzas, was written the same year as the ode, and published in *Posthumous Poems*.

Ode to Naples, published with *Posthumous Poems*, 1824, and dated by Mrs. Shelley in her diary August 25, 1820, was written, like *Hellas*, at a time of enthusiasm, on hearing of the insurrection at Naples against the Bourbon dynasty. In the "introductory *Epodes*" (so called by Shelley, though *Epode* means properly an *after*-song) he makes use of his reminiscences of Pompeii and Baiæ, where he imagines him-self inspired by an oracular voice (comp. *Ode to Liberty*, stanza i.), to which he gives utterance. In a succession of *strophes* and *antistrophes* he cries "All hail" to Naples, where the spirit of freedom is abroad. The two last *Epodes* contain a description of the march of the "Anarchs of the North" (comp. *Lines written among the Euganean Hills*, where Austria is called the "Celtic Anarch") to repress the revolution, and an invocation of the spirit of Love to keep Naples free.

To —— ("I fear thy kisses, gentle maiden"), published in *Posthumous Poems*, 1824.

Song of Proserpine, first printed in Mrs. Shelley's first edition, 1839.

Fiordispina, a fragmentary poem, probably written late in 1820, when Shelley became acquainted with Emilia Viviani. Part of it was published in *Posthumous Poems*, under title of *A Fragment* ("They were two cousins"); the rest was added in *Relics of Shelley*, 1862. Some lines originally in *Fiordispina* were transferred to *Epipsychidion*.

Lines to a Reviewer, published in *Posthumous Poems* (comp. the *Lines to a Critic*, p. 82).

Good Night, published in *Posthumous Poems*, 1824, and dated 1821. But there is another version which can be traced back to 1820. There is also an Italian version, published by Medwin in 1834, and reproduced in his *Life of Shelley*.

The World's Wanderers, published in *Posthumous Poems*, 1824. A fourth stanza, to balance the third, seems to have been lost.

Sonnet ("Ye hasten to the dead"), published in *Posthumous Poems*, 1824, illustrates Shelley's state of suspended judgment on the question of future life.

Autumn: a Dirge, published in *Posthumous Poems*, 1824. Comp. the *Dirge for the Year* (1821).

1821.—*To E—— V——*, so headed in *Posthumous Poems*, 1824. These lines, addressed to Emilia Viviani, were doubtless written early in 1821 (vide *Epipsychidion*).

From the Arabic, an Imitation. *Posthumous Poems*, 1824. Said by Medwin to be derived from *Antar*, a Bedoween Romance.

To Night, an invocation of the spirit of night, published in *Posthumous Poems*, 1824.

The Fugitives, *Posthumous Poems*, 1824, deals with a story like that of Campbell's *Lord Ullin's Daughter*, but in a far more imaginative manner. In the account of the storm we have doubtless a reminiscence of Shelley's experiences in his boat.

Ginevra, a fragment in rhyming heroics, written at Pisa, 1821, and published in *Posthumous Poems*, 1824, was part of a poem Shelley had in mind, based on a story in a book called *L'Osservatore Fiorentino*. Ginevra, who has just been married to Gherardi by her parents' compulsion, meets her lover Antonio, who upbraids her. The same evening she is found lifeless. Here Shelley's fragment ends; but it appears from the original story that Ginevra was in reality not dead but in a trance, and that she was subsequently united to her lover. Leigh Hunt's drama, *A Legend of Florence*, treats of the same story, and Shelley's *Ginevra* is referred to in the preface.

The Aziola, published in *The Keepsake*, 1829, and Mrs. Shelley's edition, 1839. Shelley's joy on discovering that the Aziola, whose presence was announced, was "a little downy owl" instead of "some tedious woman," is one instance out of many of his dislike of ordinary "society." He spoke to Trelawny of the torture of "being bored to death by idle ladies and gentlemen."

The Boat on the Serchio was mostly published in *Posthumous Poems*, 1824, but completed in Rossetti's edition, 1870. Melchior (Williams) and Lionel (Shelley) converse about their boat on the Serchio, a river to the north of the Arno, with which it was connected by a canal. In this poem we have an instance of the great simplicity of treatment that marked Shelley's later style. There is an interesting reference to his schooldays, the only one in which he directly mentions Eton.

To Edward Williams. These lines, which were included

in Mrs. Shelley's edition, 1839, headed *Stanzas*, had been published in a piratical edition in 1834, and perhaps still earlier in some periodical. In some editions they are headed *To* ——. They were written by Shelley at Bagni di Pisa, and sent, with a letter, to his friend Williams, then staying at Pugnano, a village four miles off. They are remarkable both for their sadness of tone and the startling directness of their personal allusions. The mention of "the serpent" in the first line, recalls the nickname of "the snake" given by Byron to Shelley. On Shelley's married life with Mary, *vide* p. 16.

Remembrance ("Swifter far than summer's flight"), of which there are two versions, was headed, in *Posthumous Poems, A Lament*. It was one of the songs sent by Shelley to Jane Williams.

Bridal Song ("The golden gates of Sleep unbar"), in *Posthumous Poems*, 1824. There are two variations from this song, one in Medwin's *Life of Shelley*, and another in a MS. play by Williams, to which Shelley contributed an Epithalamium.

The following lyrics were also written in 1821, and published in *Posthumous Poems*, 1824: *Time* ("Unfathomable sea"); *Song* ("Rarely, rarely, comest thou"); *Mutability: A Lament* ("O World; O Life; O Time"); *Dirge for the Year; Evening, Ponte a Mare, Pisa; Music* ("I pant for the music that is divine."); *To* —— ("Music, when soft voices die"); *To* —— ("One word is too often profaned"); *To* —— ("When passion's trance is overpast"). Several of the last-mentioned were addressed to Jane Williams.

For chief lyrics in *Hellas*, vide p. 72.

1822.—*The Zucca*, a fragment in *ottava rima*, written at Pisa, January 22, 1822; published in *Posthumous Poems*, 1824. It describes how Shelley found a frost-nipt Zucca (gourd) and revived it in the warmth of his chamber. In this there is a striking resemblance to the last part of the *Fragments of an Unfinished Drama*, written about the same time. (Comp. also *The Witch of Atlas*, stanzas 3², 33.) The opening stanzas of *The Zucca* contain Shelley's most direct exposition of his doctrine of ideal love, and furnish a key to the right understanding of *Alastor, Hymn to Intellectual Beauty, Epipsychidion*, and kindred poems. The third stanza should be compared with a passage in a letter to Hogg written as early as 1811. "Do I love the person, the embodied identity, if I may be allowed the expression? No; I love what is superior, what is excellent, or what I conceive to be so."

The Magnetic Lady to her Patient, first published in Medwin's *Shelley Papers*, 1833. The Magnetic Lady is Jane Williams; the Patient, Shelley. Some light is thrown on the subject by Medwin's Memoir prefixed to *Shelley Papers*, from which it appears that Shelley was mesmerised by Medwin and afterwards by Mrs. Williams (comp. *Lines written in the Bay of Lerici*, 15–18). The poem is another instance of the remarkable directness and simplicity of Shelley's later lyrics.

To a Lady with a Guitar, written at Pisa early in 1822. The second part (lines 42–90) was published in *The Athenæum*, 1832, the first part in *Fraser*, January 1833; the whole was given in Mrs. Shelley's edition, 1839. The MS. title is *With a Guitar, to Jane*. The characters are borrowed from Shakspere's *Tempest*. Ariel was already a nickname for Shelley in his circle of friends at Pisa, Miranda is Jane, Ferdinand is Edward Williams. Trelawny accompanied Shelley to Leghorn to purchase the guitar as a present to Jane, and also gives an account of finding Shelley writing this poem in the pine forest near Pisa (*Records of Shelley*, i. 107).

To Jane: The Invitation, written at Pisa, in February 1822. Part of it was combined with part of *The Recollection* in the *Posthumous Poems*, 1824, headed *The Pine Forest of the Cascine near Pisa;* the complete poem not being published till the second edition of 1839. It is an

invitation to Jane Williams to visit Shelley's favourite
haunts in the neighbourhood of Pisa, the pine forests and
the sandy flats near the sea. Trelawny says of him that
"when compelled to take up his quarters in a town, he
every morning, with the instinct that guides the water-birds,
fled to the nearest lake, river, or sea-shore."

To June : The Recollection, was partly given among the
Posthumous Poems ; completed in 1839. In this poem,
which is a sequel to *The Invitation*, Shelley describes how he
wandered with Jane Williams through the Pisan pine forests,
of which scenery this is his fullest description. (Comp.
Trelawny's account, vol. i. 102, 104.) By "*S*——" in the
last line but one Shelley's name was of course intended, now
printed in full in Rossetti's and Forman's editions.

Lines written in the Bay of Lerici, probably written early
in May 1822. The poem remained unknown, till discovered by Dr. Garnett and published by him in *Macmillan*
and *Relics of Shelley*, 1862. It is another of the lyrics
inspired by the sympathy of Jane Williams, whose magnetic
influence is referred to in lines 15–18 (comp. *The Magnetic
Lady to her Patient*). In the closing sentences the scenery
of the Bay of Spezzia is described. Lerici is a town in this
bay, near which was the Casa Magni, Shelley's last dwelling-
place.

To Jane ("The keen stars were twinkling") was published,
without the first stanza, in *The Athenæum* and *Shelley
Papers*, 1832, and completed in Mrs. Shelley's second edition, 1839, under title *To ——*, with the name Jane omitted
in line 3. The guitar here mentioned is presumably the
one immortalised in *To a Lady, with a Guitar*.

Lines ("When the lamp is shattered"), another of the
lyrics addressed to Jane, *A Dirge* ("Rough wind"), and
The Isle were all published with the *Posthumous Poems*,
1824. The *Song* ("A widow bird"), published at the same
time, belongs properly to *Charles the First*, scene 5.

IV. Satirical and Political Poems.

(1.) *Peter Bell the Third* was written between May and November 1819, probably at the Villa Valsovano, Leghorn. It was sent to Leigh Hunt for anonymous publication, but did not appear till Mrs. Shelley published it in her second edition of 1839. She describes it in her *Note* as an ideal poem, suggested by a critique on Wordsworth's *Peter Bell;* but one cannot doubt that it was also a direct satire on Wordsworth himself, whom Shelley, in spite of his real admiration of his poetical genius, regarded as a typical instance of political self-seeking and tergiversation (vide *Sonnet to Wordsworth,* 1816, and dedication of *The Witch of Atlas.* Comp. Browning's poem, *A Lost Leader*). The dulness of Wordsworth's later writings is also ridiculed in this "long wild laugh of a young Greek god at the vision of a highly respectable English Sunday-school teacher toiling up Parnassus." *Peter Bell the Third* purports to be written by "Miching Mallecho, Esq." (*i.e.,* secret mischief, *Hamlet,* act iii. scene 2), and is dedicated to "Thomas Brown, Esq., the younger, H. F." (*i.e.,* Moore, the poet, who wrote *The Fudge Family* under this title. H.F. = Historian of the Fudges (?)) In the concluding sentence of the Dedication, Macaulay's famous picture of the New Zealander standing on the ruins of London Bridge is curiously anticipated. Shelley's poem is called *Peter Bell the Third* because it was preceded by (1) *Peter Bell, a Lyrical Ballad,* by J. H. Reynolds, a clever skit on Wordsworth, which appeared between the advertisement and actual publication of the true Peter; (2) *Peter Bell,* by Wordsworth himself. This succession of Peters is alluded to in Shelley's Prologue. Wordsworth's poem left Peter a reformed character, and Shelley starts from this point.

Summary.—Part I. Death. Peter, now grown old, falls sick, and is persuaded by his friends that he is predestined to damnation. He dies. *Part II. The Devil.* Peter, now dead, accepts the livery, and enters the service of the devil (spirit of selfishness). *Part III. Hell.* Under this title London life is described, with its follies, crimes, and injustice. *Part IV. Sin.* Peter's character rapidly degenerates. The Prince Regent is satirised under the character of the Devil. *Part V. Grace.* The conversation of "a mighty poet" (Coleridge) rouses Peter to become an author, and he therefore gives warning to his master, the Devil. *Part VI. Damnation.* The critics set upon Peter. He finds the way to appease them is to praise tyranny and write odes to the devil. *Part VII. Double damnation.* The Devil obtains a sinecure for Peter, and himself dies. Peter is now afflicted with the malady of exceeding dulness, a "drowsy curse" which infects all about him (comp. the close of Pope's *Dunciad*).

On Shelley's satirical powers, *vide* p. 39.

(2.) *The Masque of Anarchy* was written at Leghorn or Florence in the autumn of 1819, and sent to *The Examiner*. Leigh Hunt, however, did not insert it in his paper, but kept it till 1832, when he published it in a small volume with a preface of his own dealing with Shelley's political views. The exact title in Shelley's MS. is *The Mask of Anarchy, written on the occasion of the massacre at Manchester.* The massacre alluded to was the affair at "Peterloo" (a parody on Waterloo) when the soldiers fired on the people at a Reform meeting held in St. Peter's Field, Manchester, August 16, 1819 (*vide* Martineau's *History of the Peace*, book i. chaps. 16, 17).

Summary.—The poet, as he lies asleep in Italy, sees a vision of murder, fraud, and hypocrisy in the forms of Castlereagh, Eldon, and Sidmouth (*vide* p. 8), with other "destructions" passing before him in procession. It is the masque of Anarchy, who himself rides last. They pass onward in triumph to London, where the maiden, Hope, flings herself down under their horses' feet, but is saved by an apparition of Liberty. Then are heard the solemn "words of joy and fear," which take up the rest of the poem. The voice of

Earth calls on Englishmen to rise, reminding them that they are many, and their oppressors few; that the true slavery is poverty, and the true freedom is plenty. Let a great assembly of Englishmen be called to demand their rights, without violence, but with passive and resolute protest.

Shelley's treatment of the subject is partly ideal, but the personal allusions are easily distinguishable through the allegorical veil (cf. the reference to the Chancery suit in stanzas 4, 5). The poem has been compared to Langland's vision of Piers Plowman, while in style there is certainly considerable resemblance to Blake. One of its strongest features is the markedly socialistic tone.

(3.) *Œdipus Tyrannus, or Swellfoot the Tyrant*, was written in August 1820, at San Giuliano, near Pisa. It was published anonymously the same year, but the hostility of the Society for the Suppression of Vice caused its withdrawal. It is a burlesque on Sophocles' tragedy *Œdipus Tyrannus*, and was intended to ridicule the prosecution of Queen Caroline, at a time when the Queen's entry into London and the proposed Divorce Bill were causing much indignation in England (*vide* Martineau's *History of the Peace*, book ii. ch. 2). Swellfoot the Tyrant, the gouty monarch, is George the Fourth, who had recently succeeded to the throne; Iona Taurina is Queen Caroline, about whose real character Shelley was under no delusions, though the king's attempt to divorce her had won the sympathy of the people. The idea of the "Chorus of the Swinish Multitude" (*i.e.*, the English populace) was suggested by the grunting of the pigs at a fair at San Giuliano, with allusion also to the proverbial Greek expression of "Theban pigs," and the dulness of the Theban climate and character. There are many minor characters and references which it is impossible to explain with any certainty.

Summary.—The scene is laid at Thebes, as in Sophocles' tragedy. *Act I.* The chorus of swine vainly entreat Swellfoot for redress and food. Mammon and Purganax (Castlereagh) discuss an obscure oracle relating to the entry of the Queen. Purganax summons his assistants, the Leech, Gadfly, and Rat (taxes, slander, espionage (?)). Then comes news of the Queen's arrival. Laoctonos (Wellington) and Dakry (Eldon) have vainly tried to repress the popular enthusiasm by force and fraud. Mammon, however, discloses his scheme of the Green Bag (in allusion to the green bag laid on the table of the House of Lords containing papers criminatory of the Queen), a test by which the Queen's condemnation is to be secured. *Act II.* In scene i. the test is accepted by the swine and the Queen. Scene ii. describes the application of the test, and the discomfiture of Swellfoot and his court. The Minotaur (John Bull) appears, and the oracle is fulfilled.

Swellfoot the Tyrant is grotesque in style, but the wit is rather forced and ponderous. Most critics consider it a failure, but it should be remembered that it was not meant to be taken as a serious effort.

(4.) *Shorter Poems :—*

To the Lord Chancellor, written in 1817, and first printed in Mrs. Shelley's edition, 1839. The poem can scarcely be classed as satirical, being a father's solemn curse on the tyrant who had robbed him of his children. The idea of Lord Eldon's false tears being like millstones braining their victims, occurs again in *The Masque of Anarchy,* stanzas 4, 5, and *Swellfoot the Tyrant,* act i., where Eldon is called "Dakry" (the weeper). The Chancery suit was decided in March 1817.

Song to the Men of England, written 1819, published 1839, is an appeal in a socialistic tone to Englishmen, urging them to refuse to toil longer for idle masters. In 1819 Shelley meditated writing a series of political poems, in a stirring and popular style, of which this and the four following are examples.

England in 1819. This sonnet, which was published in

1839, tersely describes the social and political lethargy of England at the close of George the Third's reign. It may be compared with Wordsworth's sonnet to Milton.

Lines written during the Castlereagh Administration, written 1819, published in the *The Athenæum,* 1832. England in this time of despair is as a mother pale from the abortive birth of dead Liberty. The oppressor is free to triumph and to wed his bride, Ruin. Castlereagh is elsewhere alluded to in *Swellfoot the Tyrant, The Masque of Anarchy,* and the next poem.

Similes, for two Political Characters of 1819, published in *The Shelley Papers,* 1833. Castlereagh and Sidmouth are referred to under various similes.

National Anthem, published in second edition of 1839—a parody on *God save the Queen,* the Queen in Shelley's poem being Liberty. At the end of the address *On the Death of the Princess Charlotte* (p. 108) there is a similar idea.

An Ode to the Assertors of Liberty was published with *Prometheus Unbound,* in 1820, under the title *An Ode, written October* 1819, *before the Spaniards had recovered their liberty.* This implies a reference to Spanish affairs, whereas the poem seems rather to refer to the " Peterloo massacre " (vide *Masque of Anarchy,* p. 94) and Shelley's doctrine of passive protest. The title was changed in Mrs. Shelley's edition.

Sonnet: Political Greatness, written 1821, published in *Posthumous Poems,* 1824, repeats the warning about the necessity for self-reform (comp. *Irish Pamphlets*).

Feelings of a Republican on the Fall of Bonaparte, published in 1816 with *Alastor,* expresses Shelley's belief that even the tyrant who could revel on the grave of liberty is not so formidable a foe to virtue as custom and faith.

Lines written on Hearing the News of the Death of Napoleon, written 1821, published with *Hellas,* 1822. The earth is represented as exulting at again folding to her bosom the great conqueror, whose return restores to her the energy which he had borrowed from her for a while. The elemental and titanic vigour of this poem recalls passages in *Prometheus Unbound*. That Napoleon's character powerfully affected Shelley may be seen by other references (vide *Ode to Liberty*, stanza xii., and *The Triumph of Life*, ll. 215–224).

V. Translations (*vide* p. 39).

I. GREEK.

(1.) *Hymns of Homer.*—*Hymn to Mercury*, written July 1820, at Mr. Gisborne's house at Leghorn, and published in *Posthumous Poems*, 1824. In a letter of July 12, Shelley says that the *ottava rima* precluded a literal translation, but that he aimed at making a readable one. It was written shortly before *The Witch of Atlas*, to which it has many resemblances (*vide* p. 67). The grotesque element of the hymn, underlaid by a certain natural simplicity and reality, was reintroduced by Shelley in his account of the lady witch.

Hymns to Castor and Pollux; The Moon; The Sun; The Earth, Mother of All; Minerva. These five translations were probably made not later than 1818 (?), and were first published in Mrs. Shelley's second edition of 1839. They are written in rhymed heroic lines.

Hymn to Venus, written in 1818, first published in *Relics of Shelley*, 1862.

(2.) *The Cyclops of Euripides*, written 1819, published in *Posthumous Poems*, 1824. The *Cyclops* is the only extant specimen of the Greek Satyric Drama. In this a grotesque element was mingled with the solemnity of tragedy. It was written in tragic iambic metre, and was distinct from comedy proper. Shelley's translation, in blank verse, is very successful, but it never received his final revision, and the text is often faulty (*vide* Swinburne's *Notes on the Text of Shelley* in *Essays and Studies*).

(3.) *Greek Epigrams.* Four translations of Greek epigrams were published in Mrs. Shelley's edition of 1839. The best known is the one *To Stella*, from Plato, the Greek of which is prefixed to *Adonais*. This translation is said by Medwin to have been improvised by Shelley in conversation with him.

(4). *Translations from Bion and Moschus.* These are interesting as showing Shelley's early liking for the poets on whose style *Adonais* is modelled (*vide* p. 70). There is a *Sonnet Translated from the Greek of Moschus* in the *Alastor* volume (1816); a *Translation from Moschus*, called "sonnet" in most editions, but consisting of twelve lines only, in the *Posthumous Poems;* also two fragments first given in Forman's edition under titles, *Elegy on the Death of Adonis,* from Bion, and *Elegy on the Death of Bion*, from the Greek of Moschus.

II. LATIN.

A Fragment from Virgil's Tenth Eclogue, published in Rossetti's edition, 1870, is the only translation from the Latin. (*Vide* p. 40.)

III. ITALIAN.

Dante's Sonnet to Guido Cavalcanti, published with *Alastor,* 1816. The translation of the companion sonnet of *Guido Cavalcanti to Dante* was probably written as early as 1815, but was not included in the *Alastor* volume, possibly because the *Sonnet to Wordsworth* was an imitation of it. The translations from the Italian include also a fragment from *The Convito* of Dante (1820?), another in *terza rima* from the *Purgatorio*, preserved by Medwin, also one written by Medwin and corrected by Shelley from the *Inferno* (canto xxxiii. 22–75).

IV. SPANISH.

Scenes from Calderon's Magico Prodigioso, translated at Pisa in March 1822, and published in *Posthumous Poems,* 1824. The assonant verse of Calderon is represented in blank verse by Shelley, who considered this one of his best translations. He remarks on the similarity of this play to *Faust*, of which it "furnished the germ." Shelley's Spanish studies with Mrs. Gisborne are often mentioned in his letters.

V. GERMAN.

Scenes from Faust (*i.e.*, the Prologue in Heaven and the Walpurgisnacht), written in spring of 1822, and published in *Posthumous Poems*, 1824. Shelley was led to this translation by seeing Retzsch's illustrations of *Faust*. He strongly felt the difficulty of the task, and said that none but Coleridge was "capable of this work." Goethe, however, is said to have expressed gratification at it. The rhymed lines of the original are translated by blank verse.

CHAPTER VII.

PROSE WORKS.

I. Essays, Pamphlets, and Reviews.

The Necessity of Atheism, the tract which caused Shelley's
expulsion from Oxford, was printed at Worthing early in
1811, and circulated at Oxford. It was the result of Shelley's
study of Hume's Essays. It starts with the statement that
all belief rests on one of the three following sources of con-
viction : (1) the senses, (2) the reason, (3) testimony ; and
proceeds to argue that in the case of the Deity none of these
proofs are available, ending with a Q.E.D. *The Necessity of
Atheism* was afterwards incorporated in the *Notes to Queen
Mab ;* the original tract is now exceedingly scarce.

The Dublin Pamphlets, 1812.—(1.) *An Address to the Irish
People,* printed at Dublin, February 1812, and there distributed by Shelley, was an attempt to show in what temper
and by what methods the Irish people would best secure
Catholic Emancipation and a repeal of the Union Act. The
pamphlet is purposely written in a popular and simple style.
It begins by stating the duty of universal toleration—
Catholics persecuted Protestants in the past, but no reta-
liations are justifiable, and the Irish demand for Catholic
Emancipation is just. Then follow repeated warnings
against violent and sudden rebellion ; the best way to insure
success is by self-reform. A second pamphlet is promised on
the subject of organisation.

(2.) *Proposals for an Association,* published at Dublin,
early in March 1812, is a sequel to the *Address,* and calls

on all philanthropists to unite in demanding Catholic Emancipation and the repeal of the Union Act. The latter question is declared to be the more serious one, as affecting the whole Irish people and not only the richer classes. Such an Association must be open-handed and sincere, disregarding the hostility of government and aristocracy, and aiming at a peaceful revolution, unlike that in France. In this way happiness may be restored to Ireland ; nor need we fear the warnings of Malthus, for the dangers he predicts would not come to pass for some six thousand years.

We cannot but smile at Shelley's youthful ardour in these Dublin pamphlets, and his idea that the Irish people, like the inhabitants of the golden city in *Laon and Cythna*, were in a mood for a philosophical survey of their position, and the prompt adoption of self-reform. Nevertheless, the moral teaching is excellent, and the political outlook shrewd. In 1824 the Catholic Association was formed, and in 1829 the Emancipation took place. Still later events have proved that Shelley was also right in considering the Union Act a yet more vital point.

Declaration of Rights, a broadside printed during Shelley's stay in Dublin, February and March 1812, the distribution of which at Barnstaple in the following August caused the arrest of Daniel Hill, Shelley's Irish servant. The "Rights" are thirty-one short statements relating to governments, individual liberty, free speech, moral rights and moral duties, religious tolerance, social inequality, and the need of self-reform. They bear a strong resemblance to parts of the second Dublin pamphlet, both being perhaps derived from a French source. Godwin's influence is also noticeable.

A Letter to Lord Ellenborough, written at Lynmouth, in the summer of 1812, and printed either at Barnstaple or London. A bookseller named Eaton had been sentenced a few months before by Lord Ellenborough (*vide* p. 8) to pillory and imprisonment for the publication of Paine's *Age of Reason*. The chief topics of the Letter are the injustice of using antiquated precedents where there is no moral offence and no crime but inquiry. Belief and disbelief being alike involuntary, morality is quite independent of opinions, and to punish for opinions is to persecute (this argument is elsewhere advanced by Shelley in *Notes to Queen Mab, The Necessity of Atheism, A Refutation of Deism*, &c.). Socrates and Jesus Christ are instanced; the latter would himself be persecuted by so-called " Christians " if he lived now. It is absurd to attempt to assist "revealed truth " by temporal punishments; truth will reveal itself. The *Letter to Lord Ellenborough* is far the best of Shelley's writings published up to 1812, remarkable alike for its grave and lofty tone, clear reasoning, and good literary style. A portion of it was included in the *Notes to Queen Mab*, and it has been reprinted in America (1881) and England (1883) on appropriate occasions.

Notes to Queen Mab. The poem of *Queen Mab* was finished in February 1813; the *Notes* were written afterwards, and issued privately with the poem the same year (*vide* p. 119). Some of them were partly drawn from earlier writings (*e.g., The Necessity of Atheism* and *A Letter to Lord Ellenborough*), while others were subsequently reproduced in *A Refutation of Deism* and *A Vindication of Natural Diet.* The chief notes are as follows :—

(1.) *On] Wealth* ("And statesmen boast of wealth "). A thoroughly socialistic note, showing the fallacy of supposing luxury to benefit the poor. Labour, the only real wealth, is expended wastefully and unfairly; the poor losing the benefit of leisure, and the rich of work.

(2.) *On Marriage* (" Even love is sold "). A protest against the tyrannical marriage-bond which chains love, whose very essence is liberty.

(3.) *On Necessity* (" Necessity, thou mother of the world "). The world is governed by an invariable law of cause and effect, in mind no less than matter. This doctrine overthrows the present notions of morality; for " praise "

and " blame," " reward " and " punishment " become mean-
ingless, except as recognitions of an unalterable fact.   Necessity is incompatible with a belief in a personal god or future
punishment.

(4.) *On Deism* (" There is no God ").   This note is mainly
a reproduction of *The Necessity of Atheism*, to which are
added some quotations from the French *Système de la Nature*
and Pliny's *Natural History.*

(5.) *On Christianity* (" I will beget a Son ").   An amplifi-
cation of parts of the *Letter to Lord Ellenborough.*

(6.) *On Flesh-eating* (" No longer now he slays the lamb
that looks him in the face ").   An argument in favour of
Vegetarianism, reproduced in 1813 as a separate pamphlet,
entitled *A Vindication of Natural Diet.*   Shelley's reasoning
that a vegetable diet is the most natural and wholesome for
man is based on the writings of Lambe and Newton, and
his own experience (*vide* p. 33).

A Refutation of Deism, published early in 1814, is a
dialogue between Eusebes, a Christian, and Theosophus, a
Deist; its object being to show that there is no alternative
between Christianity and Atheism.   Eusebes, alarmed for
the spiritual welfare of his friend, begs Theosophus to re-
consider his heterodox opinions, to which Theosophus replies
by criticising the evidence of Christianity.   Eusebes, assum-
ing the part of a rationalist, shows that the same difficulties
attend a belief in Deism, and that there is no middle course
between accepting revealed religion and disbelieving the
existence of a deity.   Theosophus, worsted in argument, pro-
mises to think of adopting Christianity.   The conclusion
that Shelley meant to be drawn from the dialogue is of course
the very opposite to that of Theosophus, " the refutation of
Deism " being another way of stating the " necessity of
Atheism."   Some of the *Queen Mab* notes are again made
use of, and Shelley again urges that " belief is not an act
of volition."   There is also a reference to the question of
diet.

Series of Fragmentary Essays, attributed to 1815 :—

On the Punishment of Death, published in *Essays and Letters,* 1840, was evidently based in great measure on Godwin's writings. Much of the reasoning is now familiar to us, but it should be remembered that in 1815 the death penalty was attached to a long list of offences, and that the more barbarous parts of an execution had only just been discontinued. The argument is as follows. The question of an after-life being insoluble, the death punishment is a vague and incalculable penalty. It is also useless as a deterrent, because (1) it makes the beholders sympathise with the criminal, (2) accustoms them to brutal sights, and fosters the passion of revenge by suggesting a connection between their own security and the suffering of others. All unnecessary punishment has a bad effect on society.

On Life, published in *The Athenæum* and *Shelley Papers,* 1832, 1833, a fragment inspired by Berkeley's ideal philosophy, and probably written in Italy in 1819, rather than at the earlier date to which it has been attributed. After dwelling on the mystery of life, Shelley avows his adherence to the belief that "nothing exists but as it is perceived." Materialism once had charms for him, as a protest against the popular philosophy, but now he had adopted this intellectual system. The distinction between ideas and external objects is merely nominal; unity is the right view of life.

On Love, a fragment attributed by Mrs. Shelley to the later period of Shelley's life, but dated 1815, or thereabouts, by Rossetti and Forman. It was published in *The Keepsake,* 1829, and included in *Essays and Letters,* 1840. After a reference to his own isolated and loveless lot, Shelley defines love as "the bond and the sanction which connects not only man with man, but with everything that exists;" perfect sympathy is "the invisible and unattainable point to which love tends." (Comp. *Alastor* and *Epipsychidion,* to which the essay *On Love* in several ways corresponds; also a passage in the *Coliseum.*)

On a Future State, included in *Essays and Letters*, 1840 : a portion of it, on Death, had been already published in *The Athenæum* and *Shelley Papers*. In this fragment Shelley advances the negative view as regards a future life (*vide* p. 27). Premising that we must lay aside all irrelevant topics, such as the existence of a deity, he describes the phenomena of death, and argues that the correspondence between mental and bodily powers indicates that both perish together. Thought is not independent of natural laws. It is impossible to show that we existed before birth; how then can we hope to exist after death?

Speculations on Metaphysics, published in *Essays and Letters*, 1840. These are five fragmentary chapters, dealing with (1) the mind; nothing can exist beyond the limits of thought and sensation; (2) a definition of metaphysics as " the science of facts," as opposed to logic, the science of words ; (3, 4) the difficulty of analysing the mind, and the right method of doing so; (5) the phenomena of dreams. The essay breaks off suddenly from a description of certain impressions experienced by Shelley at Oxford in reference to a particular dream, the recollection of which caused him to be " overcome by thrilling horror." Mrs. Shelley also records the occasion in her notes.

Speculations on Morals, published in *Essays and Letters*, 1840. Shelley meditated a greater work on morals, for which the " Speculations," written about 1815, were fragmentary notes. They are full of deep thought, and very characteristic of Shelley. He shows that happiness is the object of human society, and that virtue is the disposition in an individual to promote this happiness. The constituent parts of virtue are benevolence and justice, the former of which is inherent and intuitive, though regulated by justice. The promotion of *general* happiness is the only criterion of virtue, the conduct of individuals being based on no uniform principle, but in each case peculiar and distinctive. Moral science should consist in appreciating those " little nameless unremembered acts" which are truly characteristic, *i.e.*, in considering the difference, not the resemblance of individuals.

A System of Government by Juries, published in *The Athenæum* and *Shelley Papers*, 1833, but omitted by Mrs. Shelley from *Essays and Letters*. After defining "government" and "law," Shelley asserts that the passions of revenge and fear influence the law towards undue severity in punishments and injustice in awards, in cases of property, compacts, violence, fraud, &c. The best remedy would be government by juries, *i.e.*, to discard old legal precedents, and trust to the fairness of contemporary opinion.

Essay on Christianity, first published in the *Shelley Memorials*, 1859; the date of writing is conjectured to have been about 1815. Shelley appears to have thought of writing a Life of Christ, from which idea this essay, the most important except the *Defence of Poetry*, may have originated. He shows that Christ's idea of God was pantheistic rather than personal, and that his condemnation of vengeance belies the doctrine of eternal punishment falsely attributed to him. Historical examples are cited to illustrate the difference between just punishment and vengeance. Christ's assertions about a future life are a beautiful conception, whether true or not. As regards Christ's character we must form a general idea of it in the absence of clear historical record; probably, like all reformers, he was compelled to accommodate his teaching in some degree to national prejudices, his main object being the equality of mankind. Unselfishness, simplicity, and frugality in private life, with wide cosmopolitan benevolence, are the best means of improving the condition of men. The cause of the failure of the early Christian community is explained (*vide* p. 32). Finally, Christ's doctrines are not merely Jewish, but allied to the best philosophy of Greece and Rome, and the attempt to establish their miraculous "originality," and to connect them with a popular religion, can only trammel them.

Marlow Pamphlets, 1817.—(1.) *A Proposal for putting Reform to the Vote,* written at Marlow, and published early in 1817, under the *nom de plume* of "The Hermit of Marlow." At this time the discontent of the working-classes had taken shape in a demand for Parliamentary Reform. "Hampden clubs" were organised in many of the large towns, the Crown and Anchor Tavern being the meeting-place in London. The object of Shelley's "proposal" was to ascertain the real will of the people on the subject of Reform. He suggests that a meeting should be held at the Crown and Anchor Tavern, at which it should be arranged to divide the kingdom into three hundred districts, in each of which an inspector might collect the signatures of those favourable to Reform. Towards this inquiry Shelley offers to subscribe £100. He concludes by urging the adoption of annual Parliaments, but not of universal suffrage; the abolition of royalty and aristocracy must be gradual.

(2.) *An Address to the People on the Death of the Princess Charlotte,* by the Hermit of Marlow, was written in the second week of November 1817, and published immediately. It bears the motto (not title), "We pity the plumage, but forget the dying bird," derived from Paine's *Rights of Man,* where it is applied to Burke. In this pamphlet Shelley unites two subjects then exciting national interest, viz., the death of the Princess Charlotte, the daughter of the Prince Regent (November 6), and the execution of three misguided men for high treason (November 7). After dwelling on the solemnity of sudden death, he asserts that the death of the three rebels was not less lamentable than that of the Princess. The increasing troubles of the country and the creation of a national debt had laid heavier burdens on the working-classes. The Government had taken advantage of the discontent to stir up rebellion by the spy, Oliver, and these three men were the victims. (This refers to the "Derby Insurrection," suppressed in June 1817, which the famous spy, Oliver, was believed to have instigated.) In conclusion the people are called on to mourn for the death of the Princess, who died by the will of God ; and still more for the death of Liberty, who was murdered by the wickedness of man.

A Philosophical View of Reform, the longest of Shelley's essays, was written in 1819, and has not yet been published, though a summary was given by Professor Dowden in the *Fortnightly Review* for November 1886. It contains a full statement of Shelley's views on the subject of social and political reform ; the most important points being his demand for the abolition of the national debt, the disbanding of the army, and the gradual extension of the representative system. These remedies are to be sought by the passive protest advocated so often in Shelley's writings ; but the possibility of civil war is boldly faced, and the right of resistance asserted when all peaceful means have failed.

A Defence of Poetry was written early in 1821, soon after *Epipsychidion*, and was first published in the *Essays and Letters*, 1840. It was meant as an answer to Peacock's article on *The Four Ages of Poetry*, which appeared in *Ollier's Literary Miscellany*, 1820; but the discontinuance of the magazine prevented its publication. Peacock had ridiculed the nineteenth century poetry under the title of the " Age of Brass." This Shelley intended to refute in a second part of his essay, which was never written. The title was doubtless suggested by Sir Philip Sidney's *Defence of Poesie*. This is decidedly the finest and most finished of all Shelley's prose writings, the train of thought being as profound as the language and imagery are majestic.

Poetry is defined to be " the expression of the imagination," and the poets, in the widest sense, are they who by language, music, dance, architecture, statuary, or painting, can express the impressions made on man in his contact first with nature, and then with society. They are also teachers and " prophets." Poetry, in the restricted sense of language, is a more direct medium than the other arts ; it may include,

also, certain kinds of prose, *e.g.*, the writings of Plato and
Lord Bacon.   The influence of poetry is pleasurable and
beneficial; its function is not to convey any direct teaching,
but to replenish the imagination, "the great instrument of
moral good." Shelley then proceeds to examine the chief
phases of ancient poetry, *e.g.*, (1) Epic; Homer and the
cyclic poets; (2) Dramatic; seen in greatest perfection at
Athens—a kind of poetry which flourishes or decays together
with the social life; (3) Bucolic; a style which marks still
further decay through lack of inner thought.   Roman literature was inferior to Greek—Rome's poetry consisting in
deeds and her dramas in history.   The ruin of ancient poetry
was succeeded by a new style derived from the poetical doctrines of Christ and the Celtic mythology.   Hence
sprung (1) the abolition of personal slavery; (2) the emancipation of women, and the poetry of chivalry and love.
Dante is the connecting bridge between the old and the
new.   Homer, Dante, Milton—these are the three great epic
poets (*vide* p. 70, and comp. *Adonais*, stanza 4).   In conclusion, Shelley shows that poetry is not only pleasing, but
also useful in the higher sense.   The world could better
spare its philosophers than its poets.   The cultivation of
mere science produces unhappy social results; but poetry is
divine, the source of thought, and consolation of life.

With *A Defence of Poetry* comp. Shelley's Prefaces to *Laon
and Cythna*, *Prometheus Unbound*, *The Cenci*, and *Hellas*.

On the Devil and Devils.   The date of this humorous
essay is not known; it was first published in Forman's edition of the Prose Works, 1880.

The *Fragment of an Essay on Friendship*, published in
Hogg's *Life of Shelley*, contains an interesting reference to
Shelley's schooldays at Sion House.   The dedication alludes
to his difference with Hogg (*vide* p. 21).

Reviews.—Shelley's review of Hogg's novel entitled *Memoirs of Prince Alexy Haimatoff* appeared in *The Critical
Review*, December 1814.   Its authorship, long unknown,

was discovered in 1884 (*vide* Professor Dowden's article, "Some Early Writings of Shelley," *Contemporary Review*, September 1884).

The *Remarks on Mandeville*, a review of Godwin's romance, and the short critique on Mrs. Shelley's *Franken-stein*, were written in 1816 or 1817, and published in *The Shelley Papers*, 1833.

The note on Peacock's poem *Rhododaphne* was written in 1818, and sent to Leigh Hunt. It was published in Forman's edition of Prose Works, 1880.

II. Letters.

On Shelley's style and method of letter-writing, *vide* p. 41. All the published letters may be seen in Forman's edition of the Prose Works, 1880, except those that appeared in Hogg's *Life of Shelley* and the *Shelley Memorials*, and those published for the first time in Garnett's *Selected Letters*, 1882, and Dowden's *Life of Shelley*, 1886. Many letters have been lost, and forgeries have been frequent, notably in the collection published by Moxon in 1852. The chief groups of letters are as follows:—

(1.) *To Stockdale* (Forman's edition, vol. 3). These are some of Shelley's earliest letters, written, 1810–11, to a Pall Mall publisher, with whom he afterwards quarrelled. They were published in *Stockdale's Budget*, 1826–27. They have no literary value, but contain interesting references to Shelley's juvenile writings.

(2.) *To Hogg* (Hogg's *Life of Shelley*). The earlier of these, written from Field Place or Poland Street, 1810–11, are on the subject of Harriet Grove's inconstancy, Shelley's crusade against intolerance, money matters, and Shelley's relations with his family. They include the famous letter about the engagement with Harriet Westbrook. Others date from Keswick and North Wales in 1812. They are all poor and inflated in style, and in some cases there is a suspicion of their being garbled.

(3.) *To Miss Hitchener.* In Garnett's *Selected Letters* six are given from a large unpublished collection. They date from York and Keswick, and refer to Shelley's first marriage and his general opinions, on which subjects they throw some light. There are a few further extracts in Dowden's *Life of Shelley.*

(4.) *To Hookham* (*Shelley Memorials*), from Lynmouth and Tanyrallt, 1812–13, concerning *Queen Mab,* the attempted "assassination," and political topics. Hookham was a publisher and an early friend of Shelley.

(5.) *To Godwin* (Hogg's *Life of Shelley,* vol. 2, *Shelley Memorials,* Dowden's *Life of Shelley,* &c.). Shelley's self-introduction to Godwin and requests for advice and direction form the subject of the earlier letters from Keswick and Dublin, 1812. The later ones refer chiefly to Godwin's pecuniary difficulties, and Shelley's attempts to relieve him.

(6.) *To Claire Clairmont* (Dowden's *Life of Shelley*). The published letters, mostly written 1820–1822, are full of sympathy and advice respecting Claire's troubles.

(7.) *To Mrs. Shelley* (Forman's edition, vol. 4). These letters contain interesting accounts of Shelley's visits to Byron, first at Venice in 1818, and again at Ravenna in 1821.

(8.) *To Peacock.* There are four letters from Switzerland in 1816, two of which were published with the *History of a Six Weeks' Tour.* Probably more were written and are lost. Of those written from Italy, 1818–22, a large proportion are narrative and descriptive, dealing with travels, scenery, buildings, pictures, Rome, Naples, &c. ; others are on personal matters, literary plans, domestic joys and troubles, friends and acquaintances. They are the most carefully finished and highly coloured of all Shelley's letters.

(9.) *To Ollier* (*Shelley Memorials*). These letters, written from July 1819–21, to Shelley's publisher in England, are specially interesting as showing Shelley's own views and intentions about his writings, his wise yet modest estimate of his own powers, and his clear-headed method in business matters.

(10.) *To the Gisbornes and Henry Reveley* (Forman's edition, vol. 4). These, like the poetical *Letter to Maria Gisborne*, are familiar and colloquial in tone, showing a keen insight into character, and much practical shrewdness. They are on all sorts of subjects—literature, business, steamboats, investments, &c.

(11.) *To Leigh Hunt* (Forman's edition, vol. 4), 1818–22, are chiefly on literary subjects and Leigh Hunt's journey to Italy to establish *The Liberal*.

There are scattered letters to Byron, Keats, Horace Smith, Medwin, and others. In Mrs. Shelley's edition of 1840, sixty-seven letters were published under the title of *Letters from Abroad*.

III. **Journals and Notebook.**

From July 28, 1814, the date of Shelley's departure with Mary, a daily diary was kept regularly by one or the other. There is, however, a break for one period of fourteen months (May 1815 to July 1816). This journal has not been published, but extracts are given in Dowden's *Life of Shelley*.

History of a Six Weeks' Tour, published by Shelley in 1817, contains a combined record of the two Continental trips made by Shelley and Mary—one in 1814, the other in 1816. The first part, arranged under headings of France, Switzerland, Germany, Holland, is the account given in Mrs. Shelley's journal of the tour in 1814, edited three years later by Shelley. The four letters which follow—the first and second written by Mrs. Shelley, the third and fourth by Shelley himself to Peacock—refer to the second tour in 1816; as also does Shelley's poem on Mont Blanc (*vide* p. 81), which concluded the volume.

Journal at Geneva, dated 18th August 1816, published in *Essays, Letters, &c.*, 1840. It deals chiefly with four ghost-stories told by M. G. Lewis, "Apollo's Sexton," to Byron and the Shelleys at Geneva.

Notes on Sculptures in Rome and Florence.—Some of these

were published in Medwin's *Shelley Papers*, 1833, and by
Mrs. Shelley in her edition of 1840. Others have been
added in Forman's edition, making sixty in all. The most
remarkable are those on the *The Arch of Titus, Laocoon,*
Bacchus and Ampelus, Venus Anadyomene, A Statue of
Minerva, The Niobe. Some characteristic remarks are scattered here and there. For Shelley's views on art, *vide*
p. 35.

IV. Romances.

Zastrozzi, written during Shelley's Eton days, and published in the spring of 1810, is a wild story, full of descriptions of caves and forests, outlaws and assassinations. It is
said to have been founded on a novel called *Zofloya, or The*
Moor; but it has also been suggested that Shelley's early
romances may have been partly translated from some German source. Zastrozzi, the hero, is a desperate outlaw,
round whose revengeful purposes the plot centres.

St. Irvyne, or The Rosicrucian, was written at Oxford,
and published in December 1810. Though it shows some
advance on *Zastrozzi* in harmony and general arrangement,
its style is even more extravagant, the situations being as
wildly impossible, and the language fully as inflated. St.
Irvyne is the name of the birthplace and family of one
Wolfstein, to whom Ginotti, the Rosicrucian, a mysterious
person of superhuman size, imparts the secret of magic.
Shelley's original in this is said to have been Godwin's *St.*
Leon, where the hero learns the secret of the philosopher's
stone and elixir vitæ. There are some songs interposed in
St. Irvyne, but of no value. It is curious to notice the ortho-
doxy of the religious tone both in *St. Irvyne* and *Zastrozzi.*

The Assassins, a fragment published in *Essays and Letters,*
1840, was written at Brunnen, on the Lake of Lucerne, in
1814, during the first Continental tour. It is immensely
superior at every point to the preceding romances, and marks
a new departure in Shelley's literary style. The title has

reference to that Mahometan clan to whom the name of
" The Assassins " was given on account of their attacks on
the Crusaders in the eleventh century. Shelley, however,
who had lately been reading about the siege of Jerusalem,
identifies the assassins with the Christians who escaped from
the city before the siege. In chapter i. he relates their
settlement in a valley of the Lebanon, the descriptions of
mountain scenery prefiguring those in *Alastor*. In chapter
ii. we see the assassins, four centuries having passed, still
living apart from the world. "Assassin " is interpreted as
meaning a freethinker, one who cuts away religious prejudice.
The next two chapters are devoted to the personal part of
the story. A youth, by name Albedir, finding a strange
being (Ahasuerus) impaled on the branch of a tree, takes
him to his home and assists him. The fragment ends in a
beautiful account of Albedir's two children playing with a
snake (comp. *Laon and Cythna*, canto i. stanzas 17-20).
There is a resemblance to Prometheus in the position and
character of Ahasuerus in this romance ; and it seems as
if Shelley here first conceived his idea of a suffering yet
triumphant humanity. Another characteristic feature of
this romance is the way in which Shelley took up the title of
" assassin," as he did that of "atheist," and used it in a good
sense. (On Ahasuerus, *vide* p. 42.)

The Coliseum, a Fragment of a Romance, written probably
in 1819. Part of it was published in *The Athenæum* and
The Shelley Papers, 1832, 1833, and the whole of it in *Essays
and Letters*, 1840. The persons introduced are a blind
father and his daughter, and a youthful stranger who meets
them amidst the ruins of the Coliseum. We learn from Mrs.
Shelley's note that this stranger would have been represented
to be a Greek, brought up by an instructress named Diotima,
and it is not difficult to see that the character was in some
degree autobiographical. There is a fine description of the
Coliseum, and a panegyric on Love, which should be compared with the essay *On Love*. ·

V. **Prose Translations** (*vide* pp. 39, 98).

Plato's Symposium, translated by Shelley in July 1818 at Bagni di Lucca, and first published in *Essays, Letters, &c.*, 1840. It is an abridged version, and its merit consists in its brilliant rendering of the spirit of the original rather than in correct scholarship. Plato's *Symposium* is the fountain-head from which Shelley drew his inspiration on the subject of Love, and the distinction between the Uranian and the Pandemian Venus, which plays so important a part in *Alastor, Epipsychidion*, &c. The *Discourse on the Manners of the Ancients*, a fragment given in *Essays, Letters, &c.*, was intended to be a commentary on the *Symposium*.

Plato's Ion, A Portion of Menexenus, and *Fragments from the Republic* were all published in *Essays, Letters, &c.*, 1840.

CHAPTER VIII.

TEXT, ORIGINAL EDITIONS, ETC.

Text.

The text of Shelley's poems is in many passages as defective or corrupt as if he were a classic instead of a modern writer. This is due partly to Shelley's own manner of writing, and partly to the circumstances under which his works were published. In the first place, he wrote with great rapidity, often with a pencil in the open air, correcting hastily or leaving spaces as he went on, and always giving free play to the eager inspiration of the moment. He would afterwards revise and complete his work, and then send it to the printer with all possible despatch in order to pass on to other subjects. He was also characteristically inaccurate in details of punctuation and grammar; but it is probable that many of the supposed corruptions in the original editions were really deliberate on Shelley's part, and the result of his peculiar method of spelling and punctuating. A second fruitful cause of variations in the text was that Shelley had no opportunity of correcting the proof-sheets of a great number of the poems published in his lifetime, which were printed in England during his absence in Italy; and when his posthumous works were edited by his widow or friends, the difficulty of deciphering MSS. was often very great, owing to the many erasures and corrections and the hasty rather than careless style of writing. In Mrs. Shelley's collected editions of 1839 there were numerous passages where the text was obviously faulty, and emendations have been freely suggested by later editors and commentators, of which some have MS. authority, while others are conjectural, and in many cases far from successful. The principle which guided

Mr. Forman in his edition of 1876, which must be regarded as the most authoritative text, was to avoid with the most scrupulous care the alteration of anything, however eccentric, which was perhaps intentional on Shelley's part, but not to shrink from correcting inaccuracies which were distinctly unintentional. (For critical remarks on the text of Shelley, *vide* Swinburne's *Essays and Studies*, Garnett's *Relics of Shelley*, Miss Blind's article in *The Westminster Review*, July 8, 1870, the writings of the late James Thomson ("B. V."), and especially the Prefaces and Notes of Rossetti's and Forman's editions.)

Original Editions.

Of the original editions published in Shelley's lifetime the prose writings predominated largely during the English period, while those which were issued during his residence in Italy were entirely poems. The following were the chief volumes :—

(1.) *Prose Writings.*—*Zastrozzi, a Romance*, 1 vol. duodecimo, London, 1810. *St. Irvyne ; or The Rosicrucian*, 1 vol. duodecimo, London, 1811. *The Necessity of Atheism*, a tract, printed at Worthing in 1811, now exceedingly scarce. *An Address to the Irish People*, octavo pamphlet, Dublin, 1812. *Proposals for an Association*, octavo pamphlet, Dublin, 1812. *Declaration of Rights*, a broadside, printed at Dublin, 1812. *A Letter to Lord Ellenborough*, 1812 (Barnstaple or London). *A Vindication of Natural Diet*, a duodecimo pamphlet, London, 1813; now very scarce, reprinted by the Vegetarian Society in 1884. *A Refutation of Deism*, London, 1814, a handsomely printed octavo, very scarce. *A Proposal for putting Reform to the Vote*, octavo pamphlet, London, 1817. *An Address to the People on the Death of the Princess Charlotte*, 1817 ; only a reprint is now extant. *History of a Six Weeks' Tour*, London, 1817 ; a foolscap octavo volume.

(2.) *Poems.*—*Juvenilia* (*vide* p. 79).
Queen Mab. London, 1813. Crown octavo; on fine

paper; 250 copies only are said to have been printed. Among copies still extant is the one given by Shelley to Mary Godwin in July 1814, and the one revised by Shelley in writing *The Dæmon of the World*.

Alastor, or The Spirit of Solitude, and other Poems. London, 1816. A foolscap octavo volume, which was scarce even in 1824. The Shelley Society issued a facsimile reprint in 1885. The poems that accompanied *Alastor* are headed as follows: Δακρυσι διοισω ποτμον αποτμον (To Coleridge); *Stanzas, April* 1814; *Mutability; There is no work, nor device, nor knowledge, nor wisdom in the grave, whither thou goest; A Summer Evening Churchyard, Lechdale, Gloucestershire; To Wordsworth; Feelings of a Republican on the Fall of Bonaparte; Superstition; Sonnet, from the Italian of Dante; Translated from the Greek of Moschus; The Dæmon of the World*.

Laon and Cythna (The Revolt of Islam). London, 1818. An octavo volume. The actual copy revised by Shelley when changing *Laon and Cythna* into *The Revolt of Islam* (*vide* p. 54) is in Mr. Forman's possession.

Rosalind and Helen. London, 1819. An octavo volume, containing also *Lines written among the Euganean Hills, Hymn to Intellectual Beauty*, and the *Sonnet* on Ozymandias.

The Cenci. London, 1819. A second edition was issued in 1821.

Prometheus Unbound. London, 1820. An octavo volume. The miscellaneous poems which accompanied *Prometheus* were—*The Sensitive Plant; A Vision of the Sea; Ode to Heaven; An Exhortation; Ode to the West Wind; An Ode, written October* 1819, *before the Spaniards had recovered their Liberty; The Cloud; To a Skylark; Ode to Liberty*.

Œdipus Tyrannus, or Swellfoot the Tyrant. An octavo pamphlet. London, 1820.

Epipsychidion. An octavo pamphlet. London, 1821.

Adonais. A small quarto in blue wrapper, with the types of Didot. Pisa, 1821. A facsimile of this very scarce volume was published by the Shelley Society in 1886.

Hellas. London, 1822. An octavo pamphlet, including the lyrical drama, *Hellas*, and the lines, *Written on Hearing the News of the Death of Napoleon.*

Hellas was the last book published by Shelley. After his death the following volumes were issued from MSS. left in the hands of Mrs. Shelley, Leigh Hunt, Medwin, and other friends :—

Posthumous Poems, 1824, edited by Mrs. Shelley. Contained most of Shelley's hitherto unpublished poems, together with *Alastor* reprinted.

The Masque of Anarchy, 1832, with a Preface by Leigh Hunt (*vide* p. 94).

The Shelley Papers, 1833, reprinted from *The Athenæum*, contained a few more of Shelley's short poems and fragmentary essays, edited by Medwin.

Essays, Letters from Abroad, &c., Moxon, 2 vols., 1840 and 1845. This was to the Prose Works what the *Posthumous Poems* had been to the poetry, and consisted mainly, though not entirely, of unpublished essays and letters. The *Essay on Christianity* was not published till 1859.

Relics of Shelley, edited by Richard Garnett, Moxon, 1862, contained some new fragments of great interest.

Collected Editions.

The chief collected editions are as follows :—

The Poetical Works, Moxon, 1839, edited by Mrs. Shelley. A second edition was issued the same year. These must be classed as the first collected editions, though they also contained a good deal of original matter.

The *Complete Poetical Works*, edited by W. M. Rossetti, Moxon, 1870, 2 vols. ; and J. Slark, 1878, 3 vols.

The *Poetical Works*, 4 vols., 1876-77, and the *Prose Works*, 4 vols., 1880, edited by H. Buxton Forman (Reeves & Turner). In these editions all the previously published writings of Shelley have been collected, and a few new pieces added.

CHAPTER IX.

SHELLEY'S INFLUENCE ON LITERATURE AND THOUGHT.

THE critic's joke on the title of *Prometheus* (" Unbound—for who would bind it?") was a fair sample of the style of contemporary criticism dealt out to Shelley's poems, while his opinions and doctrines were still more recklessly misrepresented by the *Quarterly Review* and most other periodicals of that time, with the exception of Leigh Hunt's *Examiner*. Leigh Hunt, indeed, was the only one of Shelley's fellow-poets who seems to have appreciated his genius, which was certainly undervalued by Byron and Keats, and entirely misunderstood by Wordsworth, Southey, Campbell, and Moore. It was no wonder, therefore, that his books, with perhaps the exception of *Queen Mab* and *The Cenci*, gained hardly any recognition in his lifetime, and that, in spite of his good-humoured indifference to the abuse of his reviewers, he became latterly depressed by lack of sympathy and appreciation. He was at all times inclined to take a singularly modest view of his own powers ; but it is recorded by Medwin that he sometimes said he looked to America and Germany for posthumous fame, or even quoted Milton's words —" This I know, that whether in prosing or in versing, there is something in my writings that shall live for ever." During the past half century Shelley's fame as a lyric poet has been firmly established, and his reputation as a thinker has also been surely, though more slowly, progressing. No clearer proof could be needed of the power and originality of

his genius than the fact that while those readers who understand and sympathise with him are filled with a personal
love and admiration unique in the annals of literature, others
regard him with contrary feelings of aversion and animosity.
He represents the very soul and essence of a revolutionary
movement which is even now only in its earlier stages of
accomplishment; and until that movement is fulfilled it cannot be doubted that men's opinions will be as sharply divided
on the merits of Shelley's writings and character, as they are
divided on the great cause of humanity which he so unflinch-
ingly championed.

(1.) *Influence on Literature.*—Though Shelley had not,
like Wordsworth, a direct school of followers, his indirect
influence on poetry has been very great. The purely lyric
element is now far more widely understood and genuinely
valued than in the days when the *Quarterly* critics could
discover nothing but "drivelling prose run mad" in *Prometheus* and *Epipsychidion*. The "lyric cry," first sounded
in full perfection by Shelley, has been taken up and re-
echoed by succeeding poets; and all recent English poetry is
indebted to the same source for greater spirituality of thought
and richer melody of tone. Shelley has also shown, above
all other poets, how entirely the true lyrist can transcend
what Macaulay calls "the irrational laws which bad critics
have framed for the government of poets;" with the recognition
of the excellence of Shelley's lyrics, one can hardly fail to
see the absurdity of that arbitrary and dogmatic system of
criticism which was the terror of English writers at the
beginning of this century. That the estimates of critics as
to Shelley's place in literature are still somewhat conflicting,
is not to be wondered at; for the lyric spirit which is the
chief feature of his poetry is by its very nature intelligible
only to those who have been gifted with an instinctive
sympathy; a right appreciation of lyric poety is intuitive,
and cannot be acquired by study. But though there are always
critics who lay their own deficiencies of vision to the fault of

a poet whom they cannot comprehend, the balance of opinion is rapidly becoming more and more favourable ; and Shelley's true position has been admirably defined by such clear-sighted and large-minded critics as Swinburne and Stopford Brooke. It cannot be doubted that Shelley will soon be recognised as occupying that important place in literature which belongs to one of England's greatest lyric poets.

(2.) *Influence on Thought.* There is a disposition in some quarters to pass lightly over Shelley's protests against all forms of prejudice and injustice, as though such protests, however justifiable once, were no longer needed in these days of political enfranchisement. But, as a matter of fact, though the contest has passed into a different phase, few or none of the main objects of Shelley's teaching have yet been realised ; and it should not be forgotten that if Shelley were living now, he would still be a discredited revolutionist, preaching a bloodless crusade against religion, property, and all the conventional notions of social morality. *Queen Mab,* for instance, is admitted to have done some service to the revolutionary cause ; but there is no ground whatever for the assumption that Shelley's socialist opinions are henceforth to fall out of notice ; on the contrary, as the struggle between labour and capital is year by year intensified, they are likely to become of more importance ; and the same is true of what he taught about Christianity, the marriage laws, and many other subjects. It is no use attempting to clothe Shelley's doctrines with the garb of social " respectability ;" it is wiser to recognise them at their real worth. On the other hand, those who cannot sympathise with his hopes and aspirations are apt to set down his views as crude and immature, a mass of wild, though perhaps well-meant, speculation ; thus ignoring the fact that during the sixty years that have elapsed since his death all the movements which he advocated have advanced largely in importance, and while some of his opinions have been proved to be true, not one has been exploded by time. The only way to a correct understanding of Shelley's doctrines .

is to realise that they are all part of one great revolutionary and humanitarian idea, the possibility or impossibility of which is still under debate, and which cannot be contemptuously disregarded as impracticable. Time alone can decide the question ; and Shelley believed that time would be on his side.

(3.) *Influence of Character.* Nothing is more striking about Shelley than the extraordinary charm of his individual character, which not only impressed the friends who knew him personally (*vide* p. 17), but continues to affect later generations of readers. This feeling has at different times drawn tributes of admiration from such different writers as De Quincey, Browning, Frederick Robertson, Swinburne, and the late James Thomson. But here too, as in the case of his writings, we find equally strong hostility on the part of those to whom Shelley's character was unintelligible or uncongenial. To Kingsley's school of "muscular Christianity" he appears, and probably must continue to appear, little better than a weak sentimentalist; Carlyle speaks of him as "filling the earth with inarticulate wail;" others again regard him as a mere visionary enthusiast; while many have been still more strongly prejudiced against him by the tragic ending of his first marriage and the delay in the publication of the true story. It is now full time for sincere admirers of Shelley to drop the half-apologetic tone sometimes adopted in speaking of him, and to recognise that there is a singular harmony between his writings and his character. His poetical genius cannot be justly estimated apart from his opinions, and his opinions, again, found a consistent expression in the actions of his life.

The chief tributes paid to Shelley's genius by later poets are Robert Browning's *Memorabilia;* sonnets by Leigh Hunt, D. G. Rossetti, and Swinburne; and *Shelley*, an unpublished poem, by James Thomson ("B. V."). Leigh Hunt's poem *Abou Ben Adhem* should probably be regarded as a sketch of Shelley's character.

CHAPTER X.

CHIEF AUTHORITIES, BIOGRAPHIES, REVIEWS, ETC.

I. Biographical.

(1.) Mrs. Shelley's Prefaces and Notes to *Posthumous Poems*, 1824, collected editions, 1839, and *Essays, Letters, &c.*, 1840, 1845, give much invaluable information.

(2.) Leigh Hunt's *Lord Byron and some of His Contemporaries*, 1828, contains a record of Shelley, brief, but very affectionate and appreciative. It was incorporated in Leigh Hunt's *Autobiography*, Smith & Elder, 1860.

(3.) Medwin's *Life of Shelley*, Newby, 1847, 2 vols., reproduced most of the information given in *The Shelley Papers*, 1833, by the same author. The style is loose and illiterate, and there are many inaccurate statements, but the book is interesting, especially the second volume.

(4.) Middleton's *Shelley and His Writings*, Newby, 1856, a work of little merit, chiefly based on Hogg's articles in *The New Monthly Magazine*, 1832, and Medwin's *Life*, but containing a little new information derived from a friend at Marlow.

(5.) Trelawny's *Recollections of the Last Days of Shelley and Byron*, Moxon, 1858; reissued as *Records of Shelley, Byron, and the Author*, 2 vols., Pickering, 1878. This is perhaps the pleasantest of all the records of Shelley, though some of the incidents look as if they were apocryphal. The second edition is less satisfactory than the first; additions being made which are very unfair to Mrs. Shelley, on the strength of the reminiscences of an author then in extreme old age.

(6.) Hogg's *Life of Shelley*, vols. i. and ii., Moxon, 1858, includes the articles on *Shelley at Oxford* in *The New Monthly Magazine*, 1832, 1833. After the publication of the first two volumes the Shelley family withdrew the materials which they had placed at Hogg's disposal, and the book remains a fragment (*vide* Preface to *Shelley Memorials*). The older part, that on *Shelley at Oxford*, is told with admirable humour, force, and directness, but the rest is pointless and grotesque, and marred by the coarse anecdotes and extraordinary egotism of the writer. In 1832 Hogg was describing a part of Shelley's life on which he could speak with special authority; but in 1858 he seems to have been quite unable to deal with the life as a whole. Some passages of the later part have a certain amount of caustic humour.

(7.) Peacock's *Memoirs of P. B. Shelley*, *Fraser's Magazine*, 1858 and 1860, have been over-rated and over-praised, but tell some important facts. Peacock, a shrewd, cynical satirist, was quite incapable of rightly depicting Shelley's character; and his positive statements about the cause of Shelley's separation from Harriet were disproved by Dr. Garnett in *Relics of Shelley*.

(8.) *Shelley Memorials*, Smith & Elder, 1859, edited by Lady Shelley. This brief but comprehensive summary of Shelley's life was published after the cessation of the work by Hogg; and, until the appearance of Professor Dowden's book, has been the most authoritative record.

(9.) Garnett's *Relics of Shelley*, Moxon, 1862, contains among other important matter some valuable remarks on Shelley's separation from Harriet.

(10.) W. M. Rossetti's *Memoir of Shelley*, prefixed to editions of 1870 and 1885, gives an admirable account of Shelley's life, with critical notices of his chief works.

(11.) D. F. M'Carthy's *Shelley's Early Life*, Chatto &

Windus, 1 vol., 1872, is a faithful but formless account of Shelley's life up to 1812, dealing at great length with the Dublin episode, and correcting various errors made by Hogg, Medwin, Peacock, and others. A special feature of the book is the merciless exposure of Hogg's "so-called Life of Shelley."

(12.) C. Kegan Paul's *William Godwin, his Friends and Contemporaries*, 1876, shows clearly the relation subsisting between Godwin and Shelley.

(13.) G. B. Smith's *Shelley, a Critical Biography*. David Douglas, 1877.

(14.) J. A. Symonds' *Shelley*, 1878. (English Men of Letters series.)

(15.) J. C. Jeaffreson's *The Real Shelley*, 1885, professes to unmask Shelley's principles and character, while it does not deny his genius. It is remarkable for its grotesque vulgarity of tone and inaccuracy of statement.

(16.) Dowden's *Life of Shelley*, 1886, gives the true story of Shelley's life for the first time, on the authority of the unpublished manuscripts in the possession of the Shelley family. It contains letters, hitherto unpublished, addressed to Mary Shelley, Godwin, Claire Clairmont, and others, and a notice of some early poems intended for publication in 1813.

Magazine Articles.—Some of the chief biographical notices are to be reprinted by the Shelley Society; among these are *P. B. Shelley*, in *Stockdale's Budget*, 1826–27; *A Newspaper Editor's Reminiscences*, writer unknown, *Fraser*, 1841; *Shelley in Pall Mall*, by R. Garnett, *Macmillan*, 1860; *Shelley, by one who knew him*, by Thornton Hunt, *Atlantic Monthly*, 1863; *Shelley in 1812–13*, by W. M. Rossetti, *Fortnightly Review*, 1871; *Shelley's Last Days*, by R. Garnett, *Fortnightly Review*, 1878; *Shelley's Life near Spezzia*, by H. B. Forman, *Macmillan*, 1880. De Quincey's Essay on Shelley (vol. 5 of his collected works) is kindly and appreciative, if allowance be made for its wide divergence

of opinion.   De Quincey had no personal knowledge of
Shelley, and his information was chiefly based on the notice
of Shelley in Gilfillan's *Gallery of Literary Portraits.*

II. Critical.

Some of the contemporary criticisms of Shelley's writings
will be republished by the Shelley Society.   Of later
notices the most important are these—Browning's *Introduc-
tory Essay* to *Letters*, 1852 ; Prof. Baynes' article in the
Edinburgh Review, April 1871 ; Miss Blind's article in the
Westminster Review, July 1870 ; Swinburne's *Note on the
Text of Shelley*, in *Essays and Studies*, 1875 ; *The Poems of
Shelley*, in *North British Review*, 1870 ; *Some Thoughts on
Shelley*, by Stopford Brooke, *Macmillan's Magazine*, 1880,
and Preface to *Select Poems*, Golden Treasury series ; James
Thomson's ("B. V.") writings on Shelley, privately published
in 1884 ; Garnett's Preface to *Select Poems*, Parchment series;
J. Todhunter's *Study of Shelley*, Kegan Paul, Trench, and
Co., 1880 ; *Shelley's Prose Works*, in the *Edinburgh Review*,
July 1886.   Many important critical remarks are found in
the Prefaces and Notes to Rossetti's and Forman's editions.

PRINTED BY BALLANTYNE, HANSON AND CO.
EDINBURGH AND LONDON.